Pregnant in the choir

Tessa J

Dedication

To my cousin Day boo I love you so much. Through this journey in my life we've laugh, listened, and cried together. Thank you so much for your support. Happy birthday pooh.

Synopsis

Kimber , Honesty, Saniya are cousins who was removed from their parents household and placed with family. When big momma and Lucinda steps up they realized they took on more than they bargained for. So doing the only thing she knew how to do she took them to church and signed them up for choir.

Lucinda always been there for those girls when the all say words they don't mean all hell break loose and Lucinda and big momma makes them learn the hard way. Fast Forward eight years later and they see each other for the first time. Can they heal from the hurt or are they still the same ungrateful little girls all those years ago.

Chapter 1 - Big Mama

With my hands clasped together, holding steady under my chin, I shook my head. My grandchildren were about to take me up out of here. I've done everything I could possibly do to make their lives easier, and it's no fault of their own.

To the right of my three beautiful grandchildren were the sorry excuses of humans, who called themselves their parents. I still am in shock at the fact that I raised not one, but two sacks of shit.

The noise in the room was so loud, I couldn't even hear myself think. I've never been so disappointed in my life. Greg, my son-in-love, who I love dearly, looked like he was about to black out. Talk about being embarrassed. Hell, I was embarrassed for him. I watched them all point blame on each other like each of their mess was clean.

"Oh hell, that's enough. Greg and Monica,

take y'all asses over there. Slogan and Duke, take y'all asses over there to the left, and girls, y'all go to your rooms upstairs, now, and I'm not asking. Move!" I shouted, looking at each party, making sure they were going to make it to their respective places in the house. I've never been so disappointed.

With frustrated attitudes, Saniya, Honesty, and Kimber took their behinds upstairs like I told them to. My vision and attention immediately snapped back to my children.

"I don't know where the hell this family went wrong. I raised you, Monica and Duke, to be better people than this, so I'm having a hard time understanding what the issue is. Slogan, I ought to beat yo ass, but I'm not gonna do it. Nah, Big Mama's not gon' do it because I'm tired. I'm sick and damn tired of everything between all of y'all. Drugs and prostitution, really Duke?"

"Mama, you don't get it—"

"Shut up. I do get it! I do get that you let your drug addicted wife, trick you into getting hooked on drugs, when you were already fighting a sex addiction. But you know what, I didn't say one word because you're grown, and

I prayed and prayed. I supported you, loved you, and I've given you all the time I can. I had to give your ass to God. I thought you were doing better, that the both of you were doing better. Now, y'all have kids, and your drugs, sex parties, and whatever else y'all got goin' on, done ruined your fuckin' kids!"

"A-men!" Monica rose and said. My head snapped in her direction so quick.

"Monica, sit your I'm not smarter than a fifth grader ass the hell down too! Because I got plenty to say to you!"

"Mama, you can't talk to us like this, you're a Christian!" Monica yelled, moving her body back down to her seat.

"Let me tell y'all somethin'. I'm a mean Christian, baby. I follow and obey God, but I'm also a black mama, who can't allow y'all to be out here actin' any kind of way."

"That's all you care about, is what other people think...you care so much about the church, the same church who couldn't help you save this house when you couldn't pay your bills, mama. You care more about the church than us, Mama," Duke said, and I know he believed every word he was saying.

"And as I recall, you didn't help me save the damn house either, and while we're on the subject of "saving" some shit, why don't we talk about your households, your families. I can't handle this anymore, and neither can you. Kimber told me about the financial problems the two of you have been having." I pointed at Slogan and Duke. "I know y'all about to lose your house and everything y'all ever worked for because neither one of you want to stop doing what you're doing. Honesty and Kimber aren't children anymore. They're old enough to understand what's going on, and they can see and hear everything. You're losing the house that your father..." I had to stop myself. My heart was breaking at the thought of what was going on.

My husband bought Slogan and Duke their home before he passed away. They were living in an apartment, two bedrooms, where Honesty and Kimber had to share the room, and Dorian thought it would be best if they had a house. He used the last bit of his savings to buy them that house.

Now, was I mad that he didn't take care of our house first? Hell yes, and I almost lost my house because of it, after his death. We thought he'd be able to work, that he'd be here with us, to make up for the financial hit we took when he drained his savings account for them. I knew we'd be ok, but then a year later, he died of a heart attack, and there was no way for us to catch back up on the payments on our house, but I tell you what. I serve a good God, and he took care of us. I've helped out enough people in my life, fed enough people, and sheltered a lot of people, that they pitched in to save my house, just in time.

But for the last labor of my husband's love to one of his children to be in jeopardy, it hurts on a different level, and at this point, it's time for me to step in.

I regained my composure and released the hand that had been resting on my chest. "I can't worry about what you do about your house, but I can worry about what you do with the girls. Until y'all can get it together, the girls are staying with me, and that's not a suggestion or a request, baby. That's a demand. I'm done letting y'all choose sex and drugs over them. I'm done letting you choose your own selfish needs over theirs. Honesty and Kimber are moving in with me."

"I didn't wanna say anything, but I'm glad

you did, Mama. Them girls been—"

I turned around and looked at Monica. She was always mouthy and talked more shit than a cow pooped.

"Monica, hush your damn mouth. You ain't no better than them. They don't pay attention to their kids, but you, you're worse! You might feed, clothe, and keep up the appearance that Saniyah is happy and healthy, but I know what you've been doing to her!"

Angry didn't even begin to explain or describe how I felt toward my own daughter. She knows I love her. I would do anything for her, but beating on Saniyah, well that was just damn unacceptable, and I didn't care what it was for.

"There's a huge difference between disciplining your children, and a whole 'nother thing to be beatin' 'em, and I'm not gon' stand by and let you hurt my grand baby. Lucinda, come on in here, baby," I said over my shoulder, to my oldest daughter. She'd taken even more than I had. This was all old to her—I was the one who was just now finding out about what Monica was doing.

"Oh, of course, your favorite child in here, comin' to save the day, huh?" Duke said sarcastically. There was a newspaper on the table, so I picked it up, rolled it up, and swatted him over the head with it.

"Watch who the hell you talkin' to, boy. I'm still your mama, and old or not, I will beat you 'til the white meat shows. That ain't abuse, that's serving justice. Both of y'all always complain about Lucinda, but I don't compare y'all. You do! Y'all so badly want to be Lucinda, but did you ever think…Lucinda didn't give me no hell because y'all were hell enough? Shit, she didn't even have time to make no mistakes because she was busy helping me raise the two of you, especially you, Duke."

Lucinda was my oldest daughter. All her life, she'd been the most well-behaved, she treated her father and I better, and she, for the most part, had her life together.

She recently got a divorce, which landed my baby right back at home with me, but she couldn't have come at a better time, considering all the hell this family was experiencing.

"So, Saniyah, Honesty, and Kimber, are all three coming to live with me. Lucinda is going to help—"

"No, I won't have her poisoning my own

daughter against me!" Monica yelled. Greg grabbed her arm, and it was a good thing too, because she was balling her fist up, like she was going to hit somebody.

"You've done a good enough job of that yourself, honey, and I know you don't think we one of them white families, where you can put your hands on the mama and it be let go because tensions are high. I'm sixty, but I ain't white, and unless you on medication for some psychosis I don't know shit about, then I suggest you relax, honey, before you see next week before everybody else."

At this rate, the family meeting wasn't going well, which I didn't expect it would. The sad thing about it was Lucinda was the one who was truly hurting the worst out of the three of my children. She was stuck in a loveless marriage, after cervical cancer left her barren, which then became a reason for her husband to leave her. If there was anyone on the planet deserving of being a mother, it's her, and she was robbed of that opportunity.

"All I'ma say is this, and then I'm taking my daughter, and I'm leaving. Excuse me, we're leaving," she stated as she looked at Greg. "I bet Lucinda does want to help raise our kids since she can't have none of her own, and that's none of our proble—"

"Monica, I'm not gonna argue with you or talk to you about what I think is and isn't acceptable. God knows I love you and Duke, and I have given everything I have to make your lives easier. I've been a second mama to you both, but the next time you speak on my womb, Mama, I'm sorry, but I'ma fuck you up somethin' terrible. I double triple dog dare you to try and take Saniyah up out of Mama's house. I'ma go to the police station and tell them AND show them the pictures of the bruises on her body, along with the text messages about you telling her what happens in this house stays in this house!"

Now this was the other part I didn't know. I'm getting too old for this shit, and I'm definitely not going to keep going back and forth. I felt awful for Greg, who didn't want to have to be dealing with this either. He didn't condone what Monica was doing to Saniyah, and he was man enough to have a separate talk with me about it. He was also honest enough with me about how he wouldn't leave his wife behind her abuse, but that he would try and get her some help. But until then, Saniya would be staying here.

Monica looked like she was about to open her mouth again, but Greg gave her a look that could clearly only be understood between them. I did my best not to get in between married folks, but it wasn't always that easy, specifically when they were your children.

"Now, I don't wanna hear another word about it. The girls' bags have already been packed at the houses. Lucinda is going to come and pick everything up, and that'll be that. Now, if y'all wanna get yourselves together, then great. I'll be here for you if you do, but if you don't, then just leave us alone and stay the hell on out the way. I'd like to keep this out of the court system. I don't want nobody payin' no child support, nobody in extra need of shit. The time to fix this family is upon us, and one day, I'ma be too damn old to fix the things that go wrong in this family. Y'all understood?"

Everyone nodded their heads. Lucinda gave me a peck on the cheek, and just as they did as children, they followed Lucinda out of the house, headed to their respective places to get their children's' things and then hopefully, be on their way to getting some help for their trauma and dramatic asses.

Chapter 2 - Saniya

"Saniya, I know you lyin'. Where the hell you think you goin'?" Honesty asked me. I just shook my head. All this fighting was starting to give me anxiety, and I wasn't about to stay up in here with Big Mama and our parents arguing like they done lost their minds.

"I'm not, I'm finna climb out this window, and I'ma go see Jovon. He's in the backyard waiting for me. I know y'all not 'bout to turn into no snitches," I said to Honesty and Kimber. They were my cousins, but we were raised so closely, people thought we were sisters, and sometimes, it felt like it, especially since our parents were trash bags.

Kimber turned her head and stared at the wall. I didn't have time for her Judge Judy ass today. Honesty, I knew she'd have my back. She heavily sighed, but when she nodded her head, I knew she was good to go. I got up from my bed at Big Mama's house and slid my phone into my pocket.

"Just say…"

"I'ma say you in the bathroom because yo stomach hurt. That'll buy you a few minutes. When you ready to come back in, text my phone, and I'll let you back in through the side door, so hopefully Big Mama don't catch you."

I kissed Honesty on the cheek and stuck one arm out the window and then my leg. It was just two stories up, but that was why I wouldn't be able to just climb back in through the window. I wasn't Spiderman.

Once my body was out the window, I held onto the ledge with my hands and then slowly dropped down to the ground, where Jovon was waiting right there to help me up. That boy was something else. His smile…lord, it took over my soul, not to mention I loved how strong he was. He's real smart too, in college, and I love the way he kisses me.

"Hey, baby, everything good?" Jovon asked as he helped me up from the ground. I nodded my head.

"Everything is perfect now. Big Mama said me, Honesty, and Kimber are gonna stay with her. I don't know why they made us come upstairs like we couldn't hear, but that don't matter. I'm here now," I said, throwing my arms around his shoulders. He smiled and squeezed my waist a little bit.

"I'm glad to hear that. Baby, you gettin' a lil' thick back there, what you been doin'?" he asked. I moved my hands up and put my fingers in his curly hair. Jovon was the sexiest boy I'd ever seen. The only problem was, my parents felt like he was too old for me.

I tried to do things the right way, by introducing my parents to Jovon. I knew from the second I met him I loved him and I wanted to be with him. When my parents met him, he'd already taken my virginity, and I don't care what nobody says, that shit, is forever between us, but they didn't like his age difference.

Every time I'd leave to hang out with him, my mama and daddy had something to say about it. Then, my mama went to beating me, with all the frustration I guess from me not listening. They didn't want me to be around Jovon, but I didn't care. I love him, and I'm not gon' let anybody tell me I can't be with him, especially not them.

Then, I started sneaking out to be with him, but my mama caught me, and she threatened to call the police on him for statutory rape. I couldn't let that happen, but I also wasn't going to stop seeing him, so I didn't. After a while, I knew she wasn't going to actually call the police, and I didn't feel bad for what I was doing. I'm a teenager, I wanna have fun, but I'm also not the average teenager.

I'm in IB classes. I'm smart as hell, got my own job, and I already have some scholarship money just waiting on me to graduate. I'm not a bad ass little kid; I'm pretty much an adult. I even pay my own cell phone. My parents just don't understand me. I didn't plan to meet Jovon, but he came through the drive-thru of the KFC I work at, and he stole my heart from the second I laid eyes on him.

Once my mama started acting a fool, I turned to my coward ass daddy to see if he would help, and like I knew he would, he chose his wife over me, so I called the only other person in the world, as an adult, besides Big Mama that I knew I could trust; my aunt Lucinda, and she's been there ever since. Talk about A-1 since day one.

Jovon lived a street over from Big Mama. My

parents never knew that, thank God, but now, we could be together anytime. Shit was working out even better than if I planned it myself.

"I don't know, I'm just developing, finally, I guess," I admitted. Everything always happened to me late. I didn't even get my first period until six months ago, on my damn fifteenth birthday. Yes, it was as disgusting and as embarrassing as you would think.

Jovon grabbed my ass and started kissing me, and I don't mean a little kiss, I mean tounging me down.

"Jo, stop. Not in Big Mama's yard."

"Shit, Big Mama ain't here right now," he said as he started kissing on my neck and roughly grabbing my ass cheeks. I was so in the moment, and I'm not gonna lie, ready to give in to temptation once again, when I heard something snap. It was a familiar sound, and it wasn't too far away.

WHAP!

My back folded, and I felt the pain of a lifetime surge through my body.

"Big Mama! Oww! I—"

WHAP!

Again, she hit me.

"OWWW!"

"Girl, shut up and get yo fast ass in the house. Let this serve as a warning, you hear me? Lil' boy, or grown ass lil' boy, stay away from my house, my granddaughter, and go get you somethin' to do, wantin' to hunch on a little girl. You sick is what it is, and I'm from the old school, baby. I ain't gon' call the police, I'ma let Thelma handle you," Big Mama said as she patted her purse. We all knew what that meant.

"You a old ass lady, you can't do—"

Jovon was quickly silenced when Big Mama took Thelma out of her purse. I couldn't even say anything because I knew Big Mama wasn't playing, and even at sixty years old, I knew she would go toe to toe with my twenty year old boyfriend. I'd heard stories about how she used to get it in with my granddaddy when they were still young. I didn't want to cause any problems, and I definitely didn't want Jovon to be a problem.

Knowing what was best for him, Jovon made his way out of the yard, and if I wasn't already nervous, beads of sweat were running down my neck, confirming what I already knew; it was about to go down between me and Big Mama.

She stood there and watched him leave. The whole time, I already knew it was about to be some trouble.

When Jovon was gone, Big Mama started heading back in the house. I got out of the kitchen window real quick and was about to try and head upstairs to get some support for the girls, but the second her foot hit that threshold, she started going in.

"Saniya Lanae, I know you done lost yo damn mind, havin' some young boy, but that's still too old for you, come to my house. Big Mama knows everything, and I wasn't born last night, baby. You can't slick a can of oil. You understand?"

She nodded her head toward me. My stomach dropped into my ass because I didn't know if she was about to give me a whoopin' or what. She'd already hit me with a switch from the tree; I wasn't about to get close enough to let her do that shit again though.

"Now listen to me, I know right now, you feel all in love, and your hormones are hypin' you up. They makin' you see things the wrong way. If that boy love you like you think he do, he'll respect your family, and he'll respect you —"

"But Big Mama, he does respect me."

"Nah, baby, you don't know what respect is because you don't even respect yourself."

"I do respect myself. Why are you saying that?"

Big Mama started laughing like I'd said something funny.

"You don't respect yourself, baby. If you did, you wouldn't be sneaking around doing something you know is for sure gon' get you in trouble, and he don't respect you or your family because yo mama done told you more than once not to be around him because he's too old. Five years don't sound like a lot of time, and for an adult, maybe somebody who's twenty-five, thirty years old, it's not, but you're fifteen years old, baby. He's in college, you're still in high school. The flag for ya should've been raised when you couldn't even take his old ass with you to prom. Now, come on in here and sat down. I got some things I wanna talk to you and your cousins about."

Big Mama grabbed me by the chin lovingly and

waited for me to start heading toward the living room. That was one of the things I loved most about her. Everything she did, she did out of love.

Once we got into the living room, I saw Honesty and Kimber sitting on the couch with smirks on their faces. I just rolled my eyes and wedged my way on the end of the couch, beside the two of them, and Big Mama took a seat across from us.

"Now, we got to lay down some rules, girls. Big Mama is gettin' old, but I ain't dead yet, and I expect y'all to abide by my rules since you gon' be stayin' here. Number one, this house gon' be clean. I don't care who do what, but y'all gon' split the responsibility. Everybody good?"

We all nodded our heads at Big Mama. That wasn't going to be hard to do, considering our parents made us clean up all the time. Well, it wouldn't be for me and Kimber, but Honesty? Ehh, that's not my story to tell.

"Great, also, I don't want y'all stayin' up all night or out all night. I don't mind you bein' with your friends, but nine o'clock during the week, has y'all name on it. We will discuss the weekend based on events, but it ain't gon' be all night. I'm not raisin' no hoes. Speaking of which, Saniya," Big Mama turned her head to me and said, lowering her face just enough to where her glasses started tilting off of her face.

"Jovon, that's a no-no. I don't want you seeing him again. At least until you turn seventeen. Now, if you still want to talk to him on the phone, I'll allow that, but you cannot see him. Understand me when I say this, I'm giving you the opportunity to at least still talk to him. All I ask is that you don't do anything stupid. Don't break my trust, lil' girl."

I didn't know what to say about that. I was happy before because we would be seeing each other regularly, now I couldn't even see him? I could've done thatfrom home, but at least she was going to let me see him. I hoped I'd be able to do what Big Mama asked me to do, but I don't know what will happen.

All I could do was say ok. I had a lot to think about, but Jovon loves me. He won't leave me. Maybe he'd wait for me. I mean, what's two years? Really just a year and some change. I'd be a senior in high school, instead of a sophomore. I'd be older and it would be cool.

Big Mama laid down the rest of the law to us,

and it was all smooth. I was looking forward to being here with Big Mama, Aunt Lucinda, and my cousins.

"Now, if you ladies would excuse me, I gotta get this laundry finished. Honesty, why don't you come with me," Big Mama said, and I knew then the heat in the house was about to shift from me to her, thank God.

Honesty got off the couch with that fake smile she always smiled. She thought we didn't know, but something was going on with her, I didn't know what, but something, and it was something big too because whenever she smiled with her mouth closed, I knew something was wrong, even if she forgot we noticed.

I love Honesty, and whatever is bothering her, I just hope she comes clean about it soon, because I don't feel like having to get it out of her.

Kimber was looking around the house, like we'd never been here before, and I decided to take my phone out. Me and Jovon had a lot to talk about, and I hoped that the earlier we talked about it, the faster we could come to some type of understanding...

Chapter 3 - Honesty

"Big Mama, how come Saniya couldn't help? She's the one who got in trouble." I pulled on the yellow crop top hoodie I had on, pulling it closer toward my body and over my hands as we walked to the back of the house, where the laundry room was. I hated helping Big Mama wash clothes.

The laundry room was so old, the boards in the floor were coming up, the washing machine sometimes stopped in the middle of the cycle, so it was worse trying to wash the clothes at night, and the dryer, it had to be run two times, because no matter what, it wasn't going to get the clothes dry on the first or second time.

"Patience is truly a virtue, baby girl," Big Mama said as she bent down and picked up the basket full of clothes and brought them into the laundry room. "Sort the clothes out for Big Mama, would you? Don't tell the other two, but they don't know how to do shit." Big Mama laughed, and I didn't mean to, but I did too, but only for a moment.

I reached into the basket and started pulling out the clothes to sort. Big Mama reached into the dryer and pulled some of the clothes out, folding them in her lap in the foldout chair, and then placing them on top of the dryer. The quiet was nice. I hated all the fighting everyone had been doing, and it wasn't just now. I mean, our whole lives everybody has been fighting, and I'm sick to death of it. Literally, sick to death.

"Honesty, baby, you alright?" Big Mama asked me, eyes full of concern. I wasn't really ok, and I didn't know if I ever would be.

At fifteen, I thought I'd be having a better life. I love Kimber and Saniya, and I know they love me, but it's not the same as having parents who actually care about you, and our parents didn't give two fucks about us. I always wondered why they had us if they didn't want to be bothered with kids. I mean, fine, Kimber was born just ten months before me, so I guess maybe they didn't have enough time to decide they didn't want two children.

As the youngest, I thought I'd get spoiled, and I

know that sounds stupid, but most of the girls I know my age, if they're the youngest, their parents shower them with love and affection, but not my parents. Nope. They were never at home, because they were always out in the streets. They thought we didn't know, but we're not deaf and we're definitely not blind.

My daddy would come home, stumbling through the door some nights smelling like he'd been swimming in the ocean, and I don't mean the actual ocean, if you know what I mean. He came home later and later, my mama, she thought we didn't know she was drinking and doing drugs, but we knew. Everybody in the neighborhood knew, not to mention, our friends at school knew because their parents knew. I've been bullied my whole life. If it wasn't for one thing, it was for another.

I'm too dark-skinned, I don't dress "girly" enough, I'm not as pretty as Saniya and Kimber. The list went on and on, and it was stressful enough. I really didn't know what to do with myself. My parents never gave me that positive reaffirmation I thought I was going to get from them, like I saw with the kids on the Disney channel and Nickelodeon and even more on Free Form. I just wondered how the hell I got stuck with them.

"Honesty, you hear me, baby?" she asked again, this time, reaching for my hand. I nodded my head, but Big Mama knew the truth.

"Let me tell you somethin', Honesty. If don't nobody love you, Big Mama love ya. Remember that, ok? I would go to hell and back for you and the other girls, too. I heard about your counseling. Don't worry, we gon' stick to that. Does it help any? Big Mama might could use some counseling herself, other from the pastor and the lord."

I knew Big Mama was just trying to encourage and love me, and for that, I would be forever grateful. But it wasn't her love that I needed or even wanted, I guess. I wanted the love from my parents, that I was owed. Why even have kids if you don't want them? What's wrong with these people? People who are supposed to be adults?

"Counseling is ok, Big Mama. Sometimes, that lady gets on my nerves. She wants me to encourage myself, but it's hard to do that livin' with Slogan and Duke. I hate th—"

"Don't say somethin' you can't take back, baby. I know a thing or two about anger and sadness, and you got to get a handle on that before it takes over your body and your life. You understand?"

I didn't understand. Why couldn't I be angry, why couldn't I be sad? I'd been in counseling for three years now, and the only thing it kept me from doing was hurting other people, but it didn't keep me from wanting to hurt myself. No matter how many times a day I tried to fight the feeling away, I still wanted to die. There had to have been something better waiting for me on the other side.

"I am angry, Big Mama. I'm sick of parents who don't do shit all day except do stuff for themselves. I get teased at school for everything, I didn't need their help any, and now we gotta come live with you. No offense, Big Mama, but I miss my house already."

I saw Big Mama getting choked up, and I instantly felt bad.

"Sorry, Big Mama, I know G-Daddy bought that house. I'm…I didn't mean to be rude."

"Oh, baby, I know. Don't worry about it, alright? Gon' and finish them clothes, and I'ma start cookin' dinner. Your Aunt Lucinda should be back any minute now. Now, since it's the weekend, I know y'all wanna move around and have a good time, but I'd appreciate it if y'all stay in the house this weekend. What you think?"

I didn't care. I only had three friends, and they were all boys. I didn't like doing the same thing as Saniya, who was sneaking out to be with some nigga who was too old, or Kimber, who's...you know what, that ain't even my business.

"That's fine, Big Mama. When are our bags getting here? I could use a good book."

"Ain't no better book than the word of God. It's one in every room of the house, even the bathroom, for when you havin' trouble with your bowels."

"Big Mama!" I screamed, laughing. She was crazy as hell.

"What's the bible gon' do for me on the toilet, Big Mama?" I asked, curiously.

"See, that's what's wrong with you young folk. Y'all don't know how to call on God when you in troubled waters, and havin' yo behind in the toilet for an hour, baby? Yo ass is in troubled waters. Call on 'em!"

"If I pray and ask God to fix my bowels and he don't—"

"Then just wait on him. He may not come when you want him, but he-e-e'll be there, right on time. He's an on time God, yes he is! Oh, on time…"

For a moment, I was cheered up, thanks to Big Mama, walking through the house singing. Maybe this was where we needed to be all along, but I couldn't be too sure.

Once I was finished completely in the laundry room, my phone started vibrating in my pocket. I pulled it out and looked. I had three messages.

Where are you?

You ok?

Please, I'm sorry…

I didn't even want to think about that right now. I was in a good mood, and there's no reason for me to be trippin' over somebody who's just as confused as I am.

Chapter 4 – Kimber

While Saniya and Honesty were cleaning, I was in my room doing my own thing. I was, until I heard Big Mama sounding off to sing. I reached behind me and pulled the pillow over the top of my head. I'm sorry, I love my grandmama, but I don't wanna hear that shit.

There is no God, and I don't care what nobody has to say. If there was a God, he wouldn't let so many bad things happen to people in the world, and I don't want nobody telling me nothing about the universe requiring balance or no shit like that. I don't know how God could let children be born or even conceived with people who don't deserve children, like my damn parents.

At sixteen, I should be being a big sister, working a job, all the normal stuff. Instead, I'm working every day at school making sure my sister doesn't get beat up for the choices my family decided to make. I love Honesty, and I'd do anything for her, and I haven't forgotten how she truly feels. I might be the only person who actually knows, I just handle it differently than she does.

Honesty and I were born ten months apart, but we look totally different. She's chocolate, wears her hair in braids, always, and she dresses like… a tomboy. She doesn't like to get her nails done, like I do. She doesn't like to change her hair-style up, like I do, and honestly, if she weren't a girl, with a period, mood swings, breasts, and if she weren't my sister, I'd think she was a boy. She was always playing football, baseball, and she always hung out with the boys.

That was another thing; I was having to beat bitches up for my sister because she was hanging out with their boyfriends, but honestly, that's where she belonged. She didn't fit in well with females, and she seemed to be happy when she was with the few friends she did have.

I'm not going to lie, coming to Big Mama's house, it kind of messes with my plans a little bit. I was supposed to be starting my job at Chic-Fil-A by the house, but now, that's way out of the way. I'll just have to come up with something different.

Really, what I want to do is become a model. I've got the looks for it and the body. I'm tall, five-foot-ten, slender figure, freckles, high-arched, thick brows, and my legs and arms are the longest things on me. I was made for the life, I just had to figure out how to get to it. That was the worst thing—having a dream and not being sure of how I was going to reach said goal.

Even if I did know how to find someone to help me, I didn't have any real support. Thank God for the internet though. When my parents did make money and they weren't spending it on drugs, they took really good care of us, and I had nice clothes…from before, and I started taking pictures and posting them on Instagram. Ever since, I've built a nice following, not nearly as many as I probably need though. I really got lucky with the captions and hashtags, since that's all Instagram is anyway.

I looked at the clock on the table, and it was three o'clock. It was definitely time for me to post. I'd forgotten with everything that was going on around me to post something, and I was thankful we had our own rooms at Big Mama's house, which made sense since Aunt Lu, my mom and my uncle lived here growing up. Three kids, three rooms.

Sliding out of bed, I looked down at what I was wearing. It was the weekend, so I wasn't trying to be flashy at Big Mama's house. I knew we'd all be inside anyway since we just got here, and we'd end up having to go to church the next day. I'd almost rather get my eyebrows ripped out than go in there, but I wouldn't worry about it until it was time.

I had on sweat pants, my hair was in a pony tail, and I had on a crop top with Crocs on. Not my best moment, but I'd still get a lot of likes. I had eight thousand followers, and I hoped soon to be at ten thousand. When I got ten thousand and I got a job to keep money in my pockets, I could become a social media fashion influencer. I got plans, and I know what I want to do. I just need to get there.

Turning my phone around and propping it up against the dresser, I began taking pictures until my heart was content, and then I posted several of the photos with different filters with a This or That hashtag to see what they liked. Within minutes, my phone was blowing up with notifications.

I smiled as I went through and tried to like as many comments as I possibly could. None of my photos were trashy. I always keep it cute, but that didn't stop perves from hopping on my page, even though it clearly said the date I was born in my bio. That just let me dudes are disusting and as trifling as I've always assumed they were.

I've never had a boyfriend, and I don't know if I want one, honestly. I don't think they're gross or that they don't have anything to offer me, but in a way, I kind of do feel that way. I'll be graduating in just a year, and when it's over, it's over. I don't want to be stuck here with my family. I have big dreams, and I'm going to see them through. If love looks anything like what my parents have and are going through, I do not want it, and I will pass, but that doesn't mean I don't still like to look when I come across someone who catches my eye.

As I continued liking the comments, I saw one comment pop up, and it said, "Must need attention."

I just knew my head was about to pop off. Who was this dude?

I went to his page, and he was following me, which was nice, but not if he was only following me to bash me. There were lots of people who did stupid stuff like that, and I wasn't here for it. I went through his pictures, his comments and his likes, and I'd be a liar to say he wasn't cute, because he was, but I don't do attitudes, and I don't do trolls either.

I quickly commented back and said, "Your mama must be blind, because you've got a face only a mother could love. You chose to follow me; you can hit the unfollow button at any time. Thanks."

I also posted the middle finger emoji to go along with it. He wasn't ugly, but I felt like only ugly girls went to the internet seeking attention. I was on the internet seeking a career.

"You don't even know me, you funny lookin' bitch." Was his response. All I could do was laugh. He was baiting me into giving him attention, and I wasn't about to do it. I'd said all I needed to say, and that was going to be the end of it.

There was a knock at the door, so social media time was over, for now anyway, because the only person I knew with the common decency to knock was Big Mama anyway.

"Come in, Big."

When she came in, she laughed. I'd been calling her Big since I could talk. It was hard for me to associate Mama and Mommy with two different people, so I just kept it at Big. She still responded and knew who I was talking to.

"What you up here, doin', girl? Takin' more of ya lil' photos? You know I heard about your uhm…Instfram thing."

I shook my head. "Instagram, Big. Instagram."

"Right, that thing you be postin' your pictures and such. What you got on there?" Big Mama asked as she took a seat on the bed. I had to think about if I posted anything that a grandmother shouldn't see, but I didn't think so. I should be ok.

I loaded up my Instagram page again and then started showing her the pictures. She nodded, letting me know which ones she liked and didn't like. She definitely had a knack for saying which ones she didn't approve of.

"Put me on there. Go 'head. Post your granny. It ain't enough of that goin' around, chile."

If Big Mama only knew there was an entire page dedicated to sexy grandpas, and she could definitely catch her one. At sixty, Big Mama was still bad as hell. She was about five-foot-six, black and gray streaked hair that she always wore in a French braid, sometimes two, ass for days, and she had this smile that was paralyzing it was so beautiful. I love her.

I helped Big Mama find her angle and pose, and then I took the picture she was dying for me to take. Then I jumped in and took some right along with her. When we were finished, I showed her what everyone was saying about her, and she didn't say it, but she was happy, and she was blushing.

"Now listen, I wanna talk to you too. Now, I know you mad at God right now, well your whole life, baby. I know your parents don't make you go to church, but listen, you goin' with me. The only way for you to get the answers you seek is for you to come to church, have some faith, pray, and be vigilant in finding your faith, baby. You know what I'm sayin'?"

I had no clue what she was saying. "I don't understand how I'm supposed to find faith in a building."

"Church ain't the building, baby. It's the people, the fellowship, it's the lessons, the hardships. Church ain't a building made by hand, honey."

That made absolutely no sense, since the word church, I mean it was literally inside of a building.

"You don't understand right now, but one day, you will. You could have church right here in this room, but I'ma raise you up in the building, so you'll have some support and somewhere to go when times get hard, and right now, baby, they hard."

Big Mama put her hand on mine. I would've argued with my parents and anybody else, but Big Mama? I couldn't bring myself to do it, and I loved her. She deserved every piece of respect for real, that anyone had to offer. However, I don't know if I'll be able to go and enjoy church. Any time we came over here, and she took us with her, I always felt some type of way. I didn't feel like I fit completely. How could I? I'm not a believer, but I would give it a try for Big Mama. She wasn't asking for a lot, and I love her. You do what you can for the people you love. Not to mention, I'm not a little girl anymore. I'm getting older, only have one more year in high school, and I could use a little help, some spiritual help, if God is even listening or knows who I am.

Big Mama patted my leg and got up to leave. "I love you, Kimber. You're my first grandbaby. We got a special bond. I'm depending on you to help me out with the girls, ok?"

Even though Honesty was only ten months younger than me, we were in different grades, and I was her big sister. It's my job to protect her along with our little cousin, who was really like our sister, Saniya. I would do anything for either of them. No matter what it is.

Big Mama left my room, and as I was closing the door, my phone dinged again with more notifications. I saw that it was the same guy before who commented. I was ready to light his ass up about Big Mama, but when I read the comment, I couldn't do anything but laugh.

Good lookin' grandmama. You got a lot to look forward to when you get old.

Thank you, Nick, I replied.

Chapter 5 -Saniya

The next morning when it was time for church, I was so tired, I didn't even want to go. I already didn't want to go anyway, but now, I really didn't want to. I stayed up all night waiting for Jovon to text me back, and so far, I'd heard nothing from him. I tried my best to do what Big Mama asked me to do, but if it was going to have him ignoring me, then I clearly wasn't making the right decision.

I'd been up for an hour, just hoping he'd text me back. I could see his read receipts were on, and he'd read the messages, but he wasn't responding. That wasn't like him, not at all. I guess I made him mad, but I was doing what Big Mama asked me to do. Now it was going to cost me the love of my life.

"Saniya, Honesty, Kimber, get y'all behinds downstairs and eat real quick before we go to church."

I shook my head and threw a private fit in the room. I didn't want to go anywhere. But maybe church would be a good distraction though. It seemed like it might help. I went to open the door, and my aunt was on the other side.

"Saniya, good morning."

Hearing her say my name, it made me feel so welcome. I loved our aunt. She had been good to us all of our lives, and she was really the one who took care of us. When I needed to know about how to conceal the smell of my period, I asked her. When I wanted to know about sex, I asked her too. She knew everything about me, how to help me, and she did everything she could to help me out. She was more of a mother to me than my own.

"Good morning, TT. What's up?"

She smiled. It was as bright as the sun. Something about the women in our family, they were just beautiful, even if they didn't feel that way.

She stepped into my room and closed the door behind me. The smile she had on her face was no replaced with a look of sadness or confusion. I don't know. I'm not actually sure what she looked like. I'd never seen her make that face before.

"Sit down, baby," she said in more of a whisper than anything else. I looked over at her, worried, but then I took a seat.

"What's wrong, TT? You're scaring me. I've never seen your face look like that."

She smirked and placed her arm around me.

"When were you going to tell me you're pregnant?"

My mouth and nose both twisted up.

"Pregnant? TT, what are you talking about?"

"Trust me when I say I'm not tryna run down your block, but, baby, listen. I told you before when you started having sex, what could happen. You getting your period, it changed things for you, and the way your body is changing, haven't you noticed?"

I mean, I had kind of noticed, but I honestly thought it was something else. I thought it was the sex that was making my body and hips spread. I thought what was going on was normal, but I was clearly wrong.

"TT, what if my body is just developing? I could just finally be filling out somewhere else besides my brain," I said, laughing, but she didn't seem to find anything funny.

"Saniya, I love you, but I've been around you since you were a baby. Don't take this the wrong way, but you not the sharpest tool in the shed when it comes to common sense. You're smart, true, but other than that…you lackin'. I think you need to take a test. Here," she said, reaching into the pocket of her robe.

She pulled out a square, pink box.

"TT, I—"

"I know you're scared, but it's better to know than not to know, and I know I don't have to tell you what's going to happen after that."

She did have to tell me, because other than having a baby, I was lost.

"You know this is going to go all types of sideways with Big Mama. She's going to be pissed off, not to mention your mama and daddy. I don't know what's gon' happen, but I know it won't be good."

Tears started swelling up in my eyes. I didn't know what anybody would say or do, but I was a little afraid of what was to come. Did I want to be a mother at fifteen? Of course not, and now that Jovon wasn't answering my texts or my calls, I didn't know what I would do. Was I one of those girls who let a nigga get my booty and then at the first sign of not being able to get any…he runs? I think I'd made a mistake.

"Hey, don't panic. Let's just take the test first and see what happens. I could be wrong, ok?"

I nodded my head and gulped. I hoped and prayed like hell I wasn't pregnant, because then, shit was going to go way left, and the future I planned for myself, I felt like I could kiss it goodbye.

As I grabbed the box from my aunt, she gave me a slight smile, letting me know she'd be there for me no matter what the results were, and I didn't know what they'd be. I thought about my period, wondering if I'd missed one, and the last one I had was kind of short. No, maybe that wasn't right. I don't even know anymore.

In the bathroom, I started unwrapping the pregnancy test and then pulled down my pajama shorts. I still had my morning pee inside of me, so the strip would get good and wet. The test ran under the stream of my pee, and I set it on the counter in the bathroom. Then I looked at the door knob, and when I saw the door was unlocked. I started panicking because my pee wouldn't stop going, but if I didn't lock the door, Kimber or Honesty were likely to come in.

I did the only thing I could think to do at the moment. I took a deep breath in, and the pee stopped. I rose from my seat and headed over to the door and locked it, quickly. I could feel my stomach about to break loose and release my pee again, so I hurried back over to the toilet and finished handling my business.

Every few seconds, I would look over at my phone and then at the test. I wish my phone was going off the way the alarm in my brain was when I saw the two lines indicating that I was pregnant. Suddenly, I felt like I couldn't breathe. Like everything around me was closing in on me.

My chest went up and down. What was I going to do? I was really pregnant, and this was turning out to be like a Lifetime movie, but I'd seen enough of those to know I shouldn't leave any evidence behind.

I grabbed the box, the test, and left the bathroom immediately. I was so shaken up, I didn't even wash my hands. I came out of the bathroom, scared to go back to my room, but I knew I had to. When I got in there, the tears fell from my eyes so easily. I showed my auntie the pregnancy test, and she stood up from my bed and hugged me. I was so disappointed in myself. How could I let this happen?

"Oh baby, we gon' figure it out, ok? I promise," she whispered as she rubbed my head and hugged me for a while, until I stopped crying.

Taking a deep breath, I tried to gather myself. This was the worst thing that could've ever happened to me, but it was all my fault. Well, me and Jovon's. He knew more about sex than I did. He should've been protecting us. I should've been protecting me.

"Gon' and get ready for church and get downstairs and eat. I love you."

"I love you, too, TT," I said through a choking sensation as she left the room. The door closing felt like I was being shut into a private hell all by myself, and I still hadn't heard from Jovon, but we needed to have a talk, and this wasn't something I could tell him through the phone.

Meet me at the church on Fifth in an hour.

Bet!

That quickly, my worst fears had been realized, and I knew then that he clearly only wanted me for my body. All he wanted to do was use me for sex? No, I couldn't let myself believe that. I loved Jovon, and he loved me. He promised.

All I could do now was hope that he wasn't lying about something like that because I was going to need him more than anything now. But how was I going to tell Big Mama without her killing me? This was about to go all types of sideways, and it was nobody's fault but mine.

Chapter 6 - Honesty

I'm going to church, but I don't wanna see you. Stay away from me, and I'll stay away from you.

Hitting the send button was the best thing I could do. I didn't need any distractions right now, or maybe I did, but not that kind. I don't know.

Everybody was moving around the house, getting ready for church, but it wasn't that easy for me. Getting out of bed was getting harder and harder by the day. I didn't want to eat, sleep sometimes, and other times I overate, over slept, and had a better attitude. I already knew I was battling depression, but I didn't want to take medicine. I felt like that was me admitting I couldn't manage my own life, and I didn't want anybody thinking that.

"Honesty, get down here and eat, girl! I know you didn't eat dinner last night!"

I looked at the door, hoping Big Mama wasn't on her way upstairs to make me come down and eat breakfast. I just wasn't hungry. Everybody don't eat all the time, but if I didn't go down, she would come up and embarrass me.

I rolled my way out of bed and headed to the bathroom to wash my face so I would be semi presentable. The first night here, like actually living here, was hard for me. I missed my parents, even though they were trash as fuck. I missed them and wished they were better. I didn't know if this was long term, but it was scary trying to figure it out.

After washing my hair and getting myself together, I went downstairs and took a seat at the table with Saniya, who looked like something was bothering her and Kimber, who was taking pictures of the breakfast Big Mama made for us. She was so obsessed with social media, it was disgusting.

"Alright, y'all eat and everybody check themselves before we get up out of here. Honesty, I know you not wearin' that to church."

I looked at Big Mama and ten down at myself. I just wanted to be comfortable, but I knew I couldn't wear a hoodie with jeans, even though I was trying to push it.

"No ma'am, go put on a nice blouse and

you can keep your jeans on."

I nodded my head and went to change my clothes. I didn't wanna upset Big Mama, especially not before church, or the rest of the day would go poorly. By the time I changed my clothes and then ate the rest of my eggs it was time to go.

The ride over to church was the way it always had been. Big Mama sang all the gospel music she wanted, and I couldn't lie, her voice was beautiful, but I could barely appreciate it because of everything that was on my mind.

I knew when we got into church Big Mama was going to make us go to Sunday school instead of the actual sanctuary, but that was where I wanted to go, so I kept walking.

"Big Mama, I'm goin' with you," I said lowly, staying close to her through the crowded church.

"No, you need to go on in there with the young folk, baby. I want you to learn the word of God in a way you can understand it.

I grabbed Big Mama's hand so she would know I was serious.

"Please, don't make me go in there, please,"

I begged.

"I know you're scared because last time you had a panic attack. You have a lot of things going on, but that's why you goin' to counselin' and need to be hangin' out with people your own age. You don't know who can relate to you, but you should give it a chance."

I had a huge panic attack last time I was in youth church. The questions, how close everyone was, and the connections everybody else seemed to be able to make, and I couldn't make one. It scares me going in there, not to mention the person who won't stop texting me.

Big Mama turned around and started talking to someone else, completely walking away from me. I could just go into the sanctuary myself, but I didn't want to sit alone. Even though I have family, I feel like I'm alone all the time. I'm not like them. They're both runnin' around, chasing after boys. I just hang out with boys. They're falling in love and have plans for their lives, and I don't have that. I ask myself all the time why I was even born.

"Honesty, girl, come on," Saniya said, grabbing my hand and pulling me toward the hallway where we would be for the next hour or so.

She pulled me so hard, the sleeve on my shirt started to droop down my shoulder. Before I could even pull it up, I heard something behind me.

"I could pull that up for you," she whispered.

I turned around, and of course, it was Brittany. I pulled away from Saniya and told her to go on, that I would be in, in a minute. The way Brittany's breath felt on my shoulder, it did something to me, to my insides.

I met Brittany the first time we came to this church with Big Mama. I thought she was nice and pretty, and we started talking and exchanged phone numbers. We even started to hang out a little bit, but then my mom and dad's problems became our problems, and I was embarrassed as hell to let her ever come over. Then I got more and more embarrassed to leave the house because of how bad my nerves always were.

The last time I saw her, she kissed me and told me she liked me, and I haven't been right ever since then. I've been thinking about her non-stop for three weeks, and I didn't want to come, because I knew she was going to be here. I don't even have anybody to talk to about this shit. Saniya and Kimber loved boys, and I do mean loved. They were both having sex, even Kimber. I know she thinks we don't know, but we do.

It also made me feel uncomfortable because I knew how Big Mama felt about gay people. She would turn her nose up at them in the grocery store, and she's a real holy roller. I know for a fact she won't accept me, and I don't even know if I'm gay. I might be bisexual. I kind of do like one of the dudes I hang out with after school sometimes, but I don't know if that's enough to actually say I like him.

Brittany though? She makes me feel some type of way in my stomach and every where else, but I know that's not right. I even kissed her back too, but I have been ignoring her since. A little bit out of shame and a little bit out of fear.

"So you just wanna keep ignoring me, or you wanna talk about it?" she asked, sliding her hands into her pockets.

Brittany was the same age as me but short, chubby, pretty curly hair, and she had a nose ring on the side, like a hoop. She was adopted by a white family, and they let her get away with murder, so she's free…like I wish I was. She's funny and always smells good. I don't know—it's just something about her that I like, but I know I shouldn't.

I pulled away from her as quickly as I could and looked around to see if anyone saw us.

"Nobody's ignoring you. I told you I need some time to think." Which was true. I did need time to figure out what the hell I was doing.

"Yeah, you said think, but how much time does that take? I don't understand what the problem is."

And that was the problem. I wasn't like her. My family was the type that could eat you up and spit you out, and I didn't want to go through the possibility of them not loving me or not being there for me because I might be gay or bisexual. I don't even know, but I felt bad because Brittany had tears in her eyes, and I knew I let her down, but I felt that way inside all the time. The shit with my parents was getting worse everyday. I'm confused about my sexuality and this family is falling apart, so I got plenty to be sad about. She'd be ok.

"I don't know how long it's going to take, and I'm sorry I didn't say anything else to you about it, but I didn't know then and I don't know now what to say to you. I like you, but—"

"Then it ain't nothin' else to it. I like you, too. Honesty."

Brittany grabbed my hand and looked deep into my eyes. I felt like she was looking deep inside of me, like she knew the things I was thinking.

"We can't hold hands in church, B. That ain't cool." I smiled, and I didn't even know why. Brittany made me feel stupid like that.

"Nah, but we can sit together."

She grabbed me by my shirt and pulled me into the room. For a second, I forgot that my sister and cousin were in here, but as soon as I saw their faces when I went to sit with Brittany, I could tell they were both upset, and that made me question if I should be sitting with her or if they already knew and didn't accept or approve of me. This is why I liked to stay to myself.

I looked at Brittany and back and forth at them, and if I had to choose, I'd choose my family, so I got up and made my way back to them. Saying I'm confused don't even come close to how I'm actually feeling. All throughout the youth service, Brittany looked really upset, but there was nothing I could do to fix it, not even try to process my own feelings for somebody else. Nobody did it for me, so why should I?

Chapter 7 - Kimber

I didn't like whatever it was that Brittany girl was tryna do with my sister. Brittany doesn't think I know, but I do, I know she's gay, even if she doesn't know it, but I don't want her to be with a girl like Brittany. I'd heard plenty of things about her and how she liked to play bitches and niggas, and if she did that to my little sister, it would be an issue. I couldn't have that.

Before church, I scrolled through my Instagram as normal until I saw a DM pop up. That wasn't unusual. Sometimes, it was normal people just wanting to talk. Sometimes, it was a creeper, so it could be anybody at this point. I went to look to see what it said, and it was from Nick, the guy from the day before.

Normally, I wouldn't even read the message, but after he fixed his comment yesterday after the picture I posted with Big, I wanted to see what he had to say, and yes, I do stalk my comments. That's part of my job.

"Sorry about yesterday, would love to see you sometime."

He was arrogant, and I could tell that from his profile and his pictures.

So....you just shootin' ya shot, huh?

At first, I just responded to see what he said, but then after he messaged me back, I was intrigued a little bit.

"Mhmm...and I'm closer than you think, too."

That shit was scary as hell. I hurried up and asked him where he was or how he knew he was close to me, and he said that he grew up in the same town as me, but he's older a little bit, and in college, which I thought was good. But I had never seen him before in my life.

The rest of the time, sitting in youth church, I texted Nick the whole time. He was telling me about how he wanted to be a teacher, and I thought that was great. I mean, I never wanted to do anything like that, but to be a teacher, you had to be pretty smart.

I'm not gon' lie either, he's handsome. Tall, dreadlocks, wears a grill. I do like 'emthugged out. I'm just surprised somebody like him would want to be a teacher. That just goes to show you can't judge a book by its cover. Even if you think you can; you can't, and I'm just hoping that he'll be willing to see past the fact that I take pictures and shit. Yeah, I do, but I'm good at it. We all gotta have something we're good at, and I do.

I talked to him the rest of the time, and I don't wanna be one of those girls, but I haven't ever met anyone like him. He's smart and smooth, funny and nice, and he's handsome as hell. I couldn't get past that if I wanted to, and he would look good on my Instagram. I said what I said.

We were so engrossed in each other, that after he said he wanted to see me soon, my whole brain turned off until I realized Saniya was gone, and that wasn't even until youth church was over.

"Where's Niya?" I leaned over and asked Honesty during the prayer. She shrugged her shoulders like I was getting on her nerves. She was looking at Brittany the whole time, and I can't lie and say I didn't feel bad. I was going to have to have a talk with my little sister so that she knew how I was feeling. I loved her and I didn't want her to be upset and sad and lonely when it was something we could work out together. Even if we had to take on Big to do it.

Chapter 8 –Saniya

To say I was sweating doesn't even begin to explain what was going on with my body. My stomach hurt so bad, and I didn't know if it was because I was actually pregnant or if it was because I was nervous. Either way, I felt like I was going to throw up and shit all at the same time. I know that's gross, but my nerves weren't acting right.

Jovon is supposed to be meeting me outside of church, and I told him I didn't have long since he wanted to take all day to get here. I knew soon enough Big Mama would be getting out of service, and if I wasn't with Honesty and Kimber, she would get suspicious.

Finally, after ten minutes of waiting out in the burning summer heat, he pulled up in a car I'd never seen him in before. Normally, when we saw each other, he caught a Lyft or an Uber or something, so I was surprised to see him driving, and in this car no less. It was a really nice car. For him to be in school, I mean, driving a brand new Honda, I didn't know how he was able to do that. Unless it was his parents' car, which he never talked to me about that. He'd told me everything about himself except for the parents thing.

He got out the car with a smile on his face, and I was excited too. I couldn't wait to wrap my arms around him. As soon as he got up close on me, I wrapped my arms around his neck and he said, "I knew you'd come around."

That moment was ruined hearing those words. Call it hormones, but I was pissed.

"So, you were purposely ignoring me to see if I'd see you if you did? Wow, I'm really tryin' hard not to fuck up, ooh, sorry God. I'm tryin' real hard not to mess up at Big Mama's, and you don't even care."

He took a step back and had a smile on his face. "I do care. I don't wanna be missin' you and shit. Plus, I done told you a hundred times, you can come live with me on campus. I'll take care of you."

He stroked my face, and I knew everything would be ok, but that wasn't possible for us to do right now. I couldn't just run off into the sunset with him. I was too young.

"Yeah, and as soon as I do that, the whole world gon' fall apart. I'm not old enough yet, but one day. Our love is strong enough to survive waiting."

At least I thought it was until the way he looked at me changed.

"What's wrong, why you lookin' like that?"

"I just realized you got an excuse for everything. We talked about you gettin' emancipated. Now you stayin' at your crazy ass grandmama's house, you could do that. You got a job, I'll help support you, and then you can come and live with me."

I love Jovon. I have loved him since the first time he pulled up in the drive-thru, but he fantasized about shit that I wasn't even on just yet. I wasn't necessarily ready to settle down, move in together, all that. I'm only fifteen. I do love him, but we're already in a situation together that we can't get out of, and I needed to go ahead and tell him, but I was afraid of how he would react.

"What you thinkin' about?" he asked, getting closer again. I hadn't spoken in a few moments, because I wanted to say this the best way, the right way, if there was such a thing.

I had my head down, thinking, and I realized no matter how I said it, no matter what I said, it would all come out the same. I'm pregnant, and there's nothing we can really do about it.

"Jovon, I'm pregnant," I blurted out. It tasted even worse coming out of my mouth than it did inside of it.

Jovon had been holding me for a moment, until I said that. He completely let me go and took a strong look at me. One I had never ever seen before.

"Jovon, what is it?" I asked, trembling, afraid of what he might say. This could be it. He might never want to be with me again. I didn't know.

"You sure?" His words didn't sound like he was upset, more so like he was just questioning what I said.

"Yeah, I took a test this morning. My auntie said she knew first because my body been changin' real fast. I didn't know anything about it."

Jovon stared at me and then he smiled. "Man, I always knew one day, I'd be a daddy. I didn't think it would be this soon, but I'm not even trippin'. I'm so happy, and we can do this. Ain't nothin' gon' stand in the way—"

Jovon wsa quickly cut off when I heard a voice from behind me. It was like no matter what I did, I always ended up getting caught and in trouble. This time, I knew things were about to get even worse.

"So, you come to church thinkin' you gon' be fast out here, in front of the lord's house? It ain't even been a day yet, Saniya. What are you doing?" she asked, and I almost fell over. I could've died. I didn't want to tell her I was pregnant yet, and I knew she didn't hear anything because if she did, she would've said something.

"I keep tryna tell you I got eyes and ears all over the place. One of the church members came into the sanctuary to tell me they saw you out here, with some boy, and low and behold, it's the same one from yesterday."

I didn't know what to say, I was distraught because I had no privacy and I couldn't even enjoy or worry about this moment in private.

"No offense, Big Mama,--" Jovon spoke up, but I knew he was about to get shut down quickly.

"Nobody calls me that but my babies, and

you are no baby. Niya, gone back in church, now."

I turned around to walk away when Jovon grabbed my arm. "Fine if you don't want me to call you Big Mama, but listen, Niya is pregnant, and it's my baby, and I fully intend to take care of our baby. We don't need you. Niya, tell her, we don't need her!"

He was practically shouting, and Big Mama was looking at me like she wanted to snap, but nobody felt worse than I did. I'd created this problem for myself, and now, there was no getting out of it.

Chapter 9 – Honesty

Two weeks had gone by and everything was getting worse. Our parents still hadn't called to check on us. At least, they weren't calling us, and when I called, I got ignored. They didn't even text us. Kimber was leaving every chance she got to hang out with her new "Instagram follower". That was just code for boyfriend, and she thought we didn't know, but we did. Me and Kimber both followed her on Instagram, so we didn't miss the comments and the follows.

Ever since two Sundays ago, things have been bad in the house and really quiet. We found out that Saniya was pregnant, and that through the whole house into an uproar. Big Mama was pissed, and she really had every right to be because she didn't think she was going to get stuck raising Niya and a baby; that wasn't really fair.

But Saniya was happy, and I was happy for her. Even Kimber was happy with Nick, the new guy she'd been seeing. I was the only one that was miserable. Since I saw Brittany at church, I tried reaching out to her. I didn't want her to think I didn't like her, because I did, but I'm just not ready to be all out and about, about it. I know she is and has been, but my family isn't built the same way as hers, and I didn't want to stress Big Mama out or make her look bad at the church. I was confused, every day, about everything.

Do my parents love us? Does Big Mama actually care about us, or does she care more about us acting out because of how it makes her look? Brittany likes me, but is this just something fun for her for now? Am I even gay? I don't know; I might be bisexual. There were so many questions filling my brain everyday, and it was starting to wear me out.

I'd reached out to Brittany, just to talk to her. I was hoping that maybe if I talked to her, I could figure some things out about myself. I wanted to ask her how she knew she was gay or bisexual or whatever she considered herself, and maybe that would help me know. Everybody else seemed so happy, I didn't want to bother anyone else with any of the questions, and since Brittany now wasn't talking to me, I felt lonelier than ever. Maybe she thought I was playing with her emotions or something, but she was the one who came in and really ruined everything for me. I already knew something was wrong with me, but she really woke whatever that something was up, and there's nothing I can do to make it stop.

Every time we go somewhere, I try to pretend like I don't see girls so I don't think about it, but I can't help it. I even find myself following LGBT pages on Instagram, licking my lips when I see certain people. It's becoming too much. The only other person I thought I might be able to talk to about all this was my Aunt Lucinda. She loved us just as much if not more than Big Mama, and she didn't have any kids of her own, so she always went out of her way to make a way for us.

It was Friday afternoon, and I had just gotten home from school. When I came in, Aunt Lucinda was sitting at the table, chopping up potatoes, and I knew she wasn't done, so she would still be in the same spot. Big Mama had gone to her evening bingo game, and Kimber was with Nick, and Saniya was in her room, probably crying because she was desperate to leave Big Mama's. Jovon had given her all the hope in the world, but I didn't think that was a good idea. There was no way at fifteen you just know what you want to do. I know I'm still figuring it out. Shit, I don't even know what I like. That's none of my business what anyone else does though.

I got up and went downstairs. School was hard enough today, and I could use some help from Aunt Lucinda. She always had the best advice, and she'd be there for me no matter what. I hoped.

When I got downstairs, I sat down at the table. She looked up from peeling the potatoes and smiled.

"What's up, baby? Everything alright?" she asked, as she put the potato down and looked up at me. I really wanted to break down and cry right there, but I knew that wasn't a good idea because then I'd never say what I was thinking or how I felt.

I put my hands in my lap and reached across the table to grab the water that was in a glass to take a sip. For some reason, my throat was really dry.

Aunt Lucinda laughed. "Must be bad, what is it?" she asked, as she grabbed her glass to the left, that was full of wine.

"Auntie, do you…do you think I'm gay?" I tilted my head to the side, waiting for her to answer. I hoped she had something to say because I didn't know what else to do.

After she took a giant sip of her wine, she placed it back on the table and looked up at me with a small smile.

"I can't tell you if you're gay or not. I don't know, baby. Do you think you are?"

This wasn't helping, but maybe if I talked more, it might.

"I mean, sometimes, I do look at girls in a different way. I don't really see boys the same way as Saniya and Kimber. Like they're running around like chickens with their heads cut off, and I don't feel that same way, at least not about boys."

"So…is there a girl you do feel that way about, since you don't feel that way about boys?"

Her eyes seemed sincere, and I knew she cared about me. I just didn't want her to tell anyone else what I was feeling.

"There's this girl at church, named Brittany…"

I opened up and told her everything. I told her about the kiss, the texts, and now how she wasn't talking to me and how that made me feel. I spilled my entire life to my aunt, hoping that she'd have some advice or know what was going on with me. Maybe it was some type of brain injury that I didn't know about.

We sat quietly for a moment, both processing what just took place.

"Well, I don't know if you're gay. You could be bisexual. Even I don't like men sometimes, and you might not have found the right one. You could be gay, but you're still so young, and with everything going on with your parents, there are just so many uncertainties. Have you prayed about it?"

Aunt Lucinda grabbed my hand, and I shook my head no.

"Why is that?"

"I just thought, well…I figured God would tell me I'm not gay, since it's a sin and all."

I shrugged my shoulders. That was the truth of what I actually believed to be true. I figured since it was a sin, that being so, God would tell me to turn away from it.

"God don't work that way baby. I think you should try reaching out to the creator to see what he has to say. In the meantime, don't worry about what anyone else might think about it, not even Big Mama. I know she can add a lot of pressure to an already stressful time."

I nodded my head in agreement. I didn't want to tell Big Mama because I didn't know what she would think about it, and I didn't want her to be upset. I didn't want to disappoint her.

"And try reaching out to the Brittany girl again, but this time, tell her the truth about how you feel and tell her why you acted that way on Sunday. I'd be upset too, but just talk to her and see what happens. If she doesn't respond, then move on. She isn't the only fish in the sea. I promise."

I knew she wasn't, but she was the first fish, and I hadn't even gotten my feet wet yet. I didn't understand what I was supposed to do beyond telling Brittany how I felt, but I hoped she would respond. I rose from the table and kissed my auntie on the side of the cheek and went back to my room to see if I could convince Brittany to talk to me.

When I made it back, I pulled out my phone and

went to her Instagram. I figured she'd blocked me from her phone when my messages turned green and they were normally blue. I was going to message her on IG but when I looked in her bio, it said taken. That was like a slap in the face.

I started scrolling through her pictures, and there was a girl all over there. They were kissing, hugging, captions that said bae and some more shit.

All I could do was shake my head. I shouldn't have been so upset, but honestly, I was pissed, and I didn't know what to do or how to get over it. I realize I might not have been moving as fast as she would've liked for me to, but damn, it had only been two weeks since church and she was already moving on. Maybe she was too fast for me. I don't know, but I didn't want it to happen like this.

I guess I was just meant to be alone, the way I always felt anyway.

Chapter 10 – Kimber

I'd been sneaking out to see Nick for a few weeks now, and it was all worth it. He was handsome and funny, and he was in college, so that was a good thing. We had such a good vibe, and he always had a smile on his face. I loved spending time with him.

Big Mama didn't really run down my block the way she did Honesty and Saniya. They were immature, had attitudes, and they didn't know how to just keep things cool.

I pretty much had a career, my head was on straight, and I'd gotten over the whole super boy crazy phase of my life. I'd done the childish drama, and now, I had me a grown man, who was so caught up in me, I couldn't help but be caught up in him.

Nick decided to take me to this new pizza spot downtown. Anyone who knew me knew I loved pizza, and it was the best thing I could ever have in my life. The pizza slices were huge and totally worth eating. Nick was in line getting our food, and he'd been up there for a while. I just wanted to make sure he was ok, so I slid out of the booth and walked up to the line, where he had his arm around this girl.

Now, I'm not the type to automatically trip. For all I knew, she could've been his friend, the sister he told me he had. I mean, she could've been anybody. Instead of flipping out, I walked up to him and tapped him on the shoulder.

"Everything good here?" I asked, smiling at the girl, who now had a frown on her face. Not that she needed to do that since she was already ugly. She wasn't the type of woman I'd expect Nick to go for since he was talking to me.

Nick quickly removed his arm from around the girl, and from the discomfort on her face, I could tell something wasn't right.

"Yeah, bae, everything is good."

"Bae? You told me—"

"Shut up, Jessica. You talk too much," he said, venom laced in his tone. At first I wasn't going to say anything but this girl obviously had something she needed to say.

"Nah, Jessica, go ahead..say what you need

to."

I stood there with my arms folded. Somebody needed to tell me something.

"Bitch, I'm not gon' tell you shit. I'm talkin' to Nick."

"And I'm talkin' to you, and who you callin' a bitch?" I let my arms fall down to my side and looked over at Nick who still hadn't said a word. He was never this quiet, ever.

"So, you not gon' tell this bitch about us, Nick? You not gon' tell her about our baby?"

"Baby? Did you just say baby?" I looked over at Jessica, just knowing she didn't say that.

"Man, let me talk to you over here," Nick said, grabbing me and pulling me to the side. I was willing to go with him until I heard something that sounded like somebody's throat was about to come out. I turned around at the wrong time and got a giant thing of spit on my face, by none other than Jessica. I didn't care what the problem was, there was no reason to do all of that.

As two black women, I couldn't understand why she'd do something like that without feeling some type of way. I was over her and her attitude.

I snatched away from Nick and walked straight up on her.

I swung, she swung, and somehow, we fell on the floor. I'm not about all that hair pulling, so I grabbed her by the neck and started punching her silly. The whole restaurant had their eyes on us, I could fee it, but I didn't care. I could've let everything go, but when the girl spit on me, that was the last straw. Blow after blow, I landed them to her face and then to her gut. I couldn't even think straight I was so mad, and why wouldn't Nick tell me he had a baby mama? That was crazy.

After what seemed like forever, we were snatched apart. I was hoping it was Nick who broke the fight up, but I was beyond wrong. It was the police.

"You have the right to remain silent. Anything you say or do..."

Nick looked at me, but he didn't seem sad or upset. He didn't even seem worried. Meanwhile, I was about to have a heart attack. I was on my way downtown, and I knew Big Mama was going to flip her shit on me. I was the one who kept things together, not made them fall apart.

I was in love with Nick. In two weeks I felt more for him than I did anybody else. I was already taking pictures of us and thinking about putting them on my Instagram. How could he put me in this position?

Jessica and I both got carried away in handcuffs, and as worried about Big Mama as I should've been, I was more concerned with what would happen with me and Nick next.

Chapter 11 - Big Mama

"Order my steps, whooooooooooooooooooooo-oooooooooooo," I sang in the kitchen, dancing around to the gospel. People think you can only dance to hip hop, that ain't right. The girls had eaten, and I was supposed to be cleaning up, since Lucy cooked dinner, which I was in the middle of doing when my phone rang.

Now, I normally don't answer after a certain time, but since I knew Kimber was out studying with a friend, I didn't want to take any chances. Big Mama don't sleep 'til everybody is at home and accounted for.

Lucy was upstairs playing Monopoly with Honesty and Saniya. I was just glad they weren't getting into any mess, since the last few weeks have been hard with Saniya and her pregnant behind. Finding out she was pregnant once we got home was tough, but not shocking. I don't believe in abortion, and I told her she shouldn't have laid down if she wasn't going to take care of the baby, but I knew she would, especially after all the hell she'd been going through with her parents.

I wanted a different life for her, she could've had one, but she clearly wasn't using protection, and she got caught slippin'. Big Mama wasn't always a good girl, but I did handle my responsibilities.

I answered the phone and on the other end, I could hear Kimber screaming into the phone.

"Calm down, what's wrong, baby?" I asked, panicked now that she'd called me from another number and seemed like she was in distress.

"Big Ma-a-ma, I-I—"

"Calm down, and then tell me what's wrong," I spoke calmly into the phone.

"Big Mama, I'm in juvenile, and I need you to come get me," she finally said after several inhale and exhales, but I couldn't believe what I was hearing.

"What happened? Are you OK? See, I told you I didn't like that Crystal girl before you left. She ain't never—"

"Big Mama, I lied. This ain't about Crystal. I got into a fight with this girl named Jessica—"

"Who's Jessica?"

"Big, please!"

I had to calm the hell down. None of this was adding up, and I didn't know what was going on.

"Jessica is Nick's baby mama. Nick is, was my boyfriend, and I beat her up at the pizza spot. Please come and get me, Big. I'm sorry I lied, but please…"

All I could was shake my head. This damn family was falling apart, and I didn't know how to put it back together. Honesty was depressed, whether she wanted to admit it or not. Saniya was pregnant, and now Kimber, the one I thought I didn't have to worry about was becoming the one I had to worry about? No, that just couldn't be.

I got off the phone with her, reassuring her that I was on my way. No matter how upset I was, I didn't want her to have to stay in a cell. I grabbed my keys, not thinking anything about saying something to anyone else, and I headed out.

On the ride over, I cut on my Yolanda Adams. I needed to be filled with the spirit so I didn't snatch Kimber bald when I finally did see her.

I got to the juvenile detention center so fast, even I was shocked at how quickly arrived. I jumped out of the car and ran up the stairs with my ID out. I pushed the buzzer and told the man on the other end who I was there to pick up. They had me wait at a counter, where the woman handed me Kimber's file. Just the thought made me angry again.

Looking through it until she came upstairs, I found out she'd beaten the girl up so bad, that was why she had to be taken to juvenile. Nobody was pressing charges thank God, but still, this could've come out so much worse.

When Kimber made it upstairs, her hair was all over her head, her clothes were a mess, and she just looked awful.

"you should see the other girl," she said, smirking.

"Girl, I know you don't think this is funny. Bring yo narrow lyin' behind on here," I said, picking my purse up off the counter, leading her outside.

The entire ride home, I didn't say a word. I didn't want to speak out of anger but out of love, and I needed to address all of my babies at the same time. Somehow, we must've all gotten our wires crossed, and I needed to know what was going on.

When we got home, Kimber practically fell out of the car. I knew she was tired, but we all had some things to discuss, to get a few things under control. I got out of the car and made my way up the stairs first. I knew Kimber would be too afraid to walk in before me because she knew I would still whoop her with no questions.

"Y'all all come downstairs, we need to have a talk!" My voice boomed throughout the house. The girls came downstairs almost instantly, including Lucinda. I knew having the girls around here would keep her in high spirits, and I couldn't have been happier. I was more concerned with what the girls were doing now that they were here.

It seemed like them coming to live here hadn't been doing them any good or doing them any better than when they were with their parents.

Everyone got seated comfortably on the couch.

"I know y'all are eager to get back to your game—"

"What the hell happened to you? Sorry, Big

Mama, but I know you see—"

"Saniya, hush, this is part of the reason why y'all are down here so I can talk to you."

I took a seat across from them, knowing we needed to have a deep conversation, and it wouldn't be easy.

"I love the three of you girls like you're my own and not just my grandchildren. It pains me when you're not obedient. Obey your mother and father, commands the lord. I'm not yo mama or ya daddy, but I've been raising y'all. Saniya, I'm not even going to go there with you, but you 'bout to have to work harder than you ever have. Honesty, I know you goin' through some thangs, and if we need to get you a better therapist, we will. Kimber, I'm not even gonna lie, I'm so disappointed in you—"

"But Big, you didn't even let me explain."

"Explain how you wasn't where you said you were going to be? Explain how you got into a fight with some girl at a restaurant? Explain what, exactly?"

She sat back in her seat and folded her arms.

"See the problem is y'all been takin' care of yourselves so long, y'all don't think you don't have to follow rules, but you couldn't be more wrong. You have to follow my rules if you want to stay under this roof. Big Mama loves you, and I'd do anything for you, but this mess won't be tolerated. This is the last warning. Next time, I'm taking phones, tv's, leaving the house privileges. Kimber, I look to you to keep things in line, not get them out of order. You're better than this, and whatever you were fighting over…it ain't worth it. I'm telling you that now."

"Big, I don't mean no disrespect, but you don't know Nick. You don't know if he's worth it or not."

I shook my head and walked over to her, placing my hand on her face.

"Kimmy, listen to me baby, any man or boy who would let you get into a spat so bad, where you actually completed a fight, ain't worth it. Mark my words."

"Big Mama, everybody ain't like you, to meet the man of their dreams the first time around. You got lucky," Saniya said. I knew she was just taking up for her cousin, but now wasn't the time.

"So that means she should settle? I know

times are different than when I was a young girl, but worth and value, them two thangs is priceless. You should never give your time or energy to somebody who ain't worth it or to a situation you don't," I said, looking at Saniya. She was pregnant and didn't want to be, but an abortion was out of the question. She thought I didn't know, but I could tell by all the things she was saying that she wasn't ready to settle down. She loved Jovon, but she wasn't ready for him to be her one and only.

"My point is, some things got to change around here, or it's gon' get real tough around here. Kimber, gon' upstairs and we'll finish this up in the morning. Lucy, please watch over them. I need to get me some sleep. They done wore me out."

I threw my hands up and walked out of the room. I didn't know how much more of this I could take.

Chapter 12 –Saniya

Being pregnant hadn't been easy. It had only been two weeks, and I already felt differently. Big Mama took me to the doctor and I was only eight weeks. I had a long way to go, but between Big Mama and Jovon, I didn't know if I was going to make it. He was begging me to get emancipated, and I didn't want to do that. I barely wanted to stay in Big Mama's house with my cousins and auntie, let alone have to do it with a man.

No matter how many times he mentioned it, nothing changed in my mind. I still couldn't get over the fact that I was pregnant, and he really wanted to be with me, but I seemed to be the only person who was experiencing confusion. I know most girls my age want a man they can love and who will give them the world, but I don't know if I was really ready for that.

Big Mama told me I could only see Jovon during doctor's appointments and to get things for the baby, but I didn't want to see him at all. Something about this whole situation had me ready to run. He was my first, and I love him, but I didn't think this would be th end of the line for me. I'm still young and want to have a good time, but I would never do to my kids what my parents did to me or even how Kimber and Honesty's parents treated them.

I decided to stay home from school today because my morning sickness had been out of control. After the weekend we all had, I was surprised Big Mama let me even stay home, but I think she knew I needed it. I was literally dying inside.

I thought I'd stay home and get some rest, but as soon as the house stopped moving around from Kimber and Honesty going to school, Aunt Lucinda going to work, and Big Mama leaving for prayer meeting, somebody knocked on the door. I wasn't going to answer at first until I heard the voice on the other end.

"I know I'm not supposed to be here, but I got some stuff for the baby," Jovon said, close enough to the door that it almost sounded like he was inside the house. Since the doctor's appointment, he'd been calling and FaceTiming me nonstop. I hardly ever answered the phone for him anymore. I tried to just text him and then leave it alone for the day, but that was almost impossible without blocking him because of how much he'd call my phone. I hated it.

Knowing I couldn't leave him outside forever, I trudged my way to the front door and pulled the door open, to what seemed like a whole Baby's R Us.

"Jovon, where did you get the money to pay for all this stuff?" I asked. I just knew he couldn't afford this without someone's help.

"I keep trying to tell you, I got it. I mean, I'm in school and I sell a little weed on the side. I need to now more than ever, especially if it'll help take care of my future wife and baby."

"Future wife?" I almost whispered. I wasn't prepared to hear that at all.

"You've gotta chill out, jovon. I'm not old enough or ready yet to be anybody's wife. I'm barely hanging on as a baby mama." Even the word baby coming out of my mouth out loud sounded horrible. What was I doing?

"You ain't just no baby mama. You're my girlfriend, and I love you, Niya."

He put his hand on my cheek and stroked it

gently. As happy as I wished I could say I was, I wasn't. I didn't want to be a wife, a baby mama, none of that. I just wanted to be my same old self with the same dreams I had before. None of this was fair.

I pulled away from him, not wanting to be touched. I saw his face twist up with confusion, but this wasn't what I wanted right now, or shit, maybe ever. I always thought I would have graduated from college and been married after that, but things were starting to feel like that was happening right now, and I wasn't even eighteen yet.

"Jovon, what's all this stuff?" I asked, once I finally got the courage to speak.

"It's stuff for our baby. I got stuff for both sexes since we don't know what we're having yet."

There were bags and bags and bags full of stuff. If this stuff were all for me, I'd probably be happy, but seeing all this stuff for the baby made things even realer, and I couldn't deal.

"Ok, Jovon, thanks. I think you better go before Big Mama comes back."

I started trying to push him toward the car but he grabbed my arm and said, "Wait."

I looked up at him, hoping he wasn't about to ask me for a kiss or some shit like that. Jovon normally turned me on, but now looking at him, I couldn't have been more disgusted with him or myself.

"I don't know how much longer I can keep doing this, Niya."

I felt the same way. Finally, he had gotten it through his head. No matter how many times I told him I wasn't ready for this, he pushed and he pushed, but I didn't want to do this. I didn't want to have this baby.

"God, I'm so happy to finally hear that you've come around. I don't wanna have a baby right now, Jovon. I think we should—"

"I know you ain't 'bout to say abortion, and that's not what I was talking about. I was 'bout to say, I can't handle being pregnant or with you. You wanna get married, and I'm just not on that type of time. I mean, maybe in like ten years, but for now, I just wanna enjoy my life, and I can't do that with a baby on my hip. This totally derailed my plans, and I don't know why you can't see that!" I shouted. I was speaking from the core with this.

"You think I planned this? You think I

trapped you?"

"Woah, I wasn't saying anything like that, but now that you mentioned it…"

"You know what, I done did everything for you, niya. I love you. Just a few weeks ago, you wassneakin' out to see me, to be with me, now you can't stand the sight of me. I don't know if this is some hormonal type of shit or what, but when you ready to be back to your normal self, let me know. I'm not 'bout to keep waiting for the person I love to love me back. I knew I shouldn't have messed with no young ass girl like you!"

As soon as he finished his statement, he turned around and left. I couldn't even believe he was talking to me like that. I was deadass speechless, but I had something that was going to fix everything for me. I knew it was going to upset Big Mama, and I felt bad, but she had to understand this was my life, and with my life, I would do whatever was necessary and right for me. I couldn't worry about what everybody else thought or felt. Nobody can live my life for me.

I was about to dance with the devil just so I could get some peace in my own life. I just hoped she really would help me.

After jovon drove off, I pulled all the stuff into the house and took it up to my room. Even though nobody was home, I still for some reason felt like I needed to close my door for privacy. Once it was closed, I started scrolling through my phone and looked for my mom's name. It literally said Monica, because I couldn't remember the last time I called her mom, but as I pressed her name, my throat felt a little stuck. Like I couldn't breathe. I was nervous, not to talk to her, but to tell her what I had to say and to hear what she'd say back. But this was the least she could do for me. If she wanted me to ever forgive her, this would be a good start.

The phone rang for a few seconds. I was about to give up when she picked up. I expected her to sound hateful on the other line, but she didn't. She actually sounded like she missed me, even though I hadn't heard from her.

"Niya, you ok?"

I stared at the phone for a second. It had been a long time since my mom seemed worried about me. She had a bad temper and was always angry. I would've called my dad, but I didn't know if he knew I had been having sex, and he would be devastated to find out the news I was about to dtop on my own mother.

"Mama, I need you," I cried into the phone. It had been so long since I was able to have a conversation with my mother, I just hoped I could trust her.

"You need me to come pick you up?"

Tears were fallin freely down my face. I didn't expect to feel this way, but I couldn't help that I did, and I didn't know how to say what I needed to. I took a deep breath, and started rambling on and on about everything that had been happening. I thought being at Big Mama's house would cure all my problems, but it didn't. It wasn't her fault—it was my own. She told me to stay away from him, even before my mama started beating on me. She told me that a boy his age either wanted one of two things; he wanted to take my virginity and bounce, or he was in it for the long haul. She warned me that I wouldn't be happy in either instance, but I didn't think that could even be a thing, until now.

"No, well, yes. Mama, I want to have an abortion," I finally said after explaining everything that was going on with me.

"An abortion?" She laughed. I didn't think anything was funny.

"Yeah, an abortion. I'm not asking you to pay for it. I'll pay for it, but I'm not old enough to legally have one on my own I don't think. I know I'm not gonna be able to get myself back from the clinic, and I need some support. Big Mama ain't goin'."

"You damn right, Big Mama ain't goin'. We don't really believe in abortion in this family."

"But it's my baby, my body, and my money. I don't get it!" I screamed through tears on the phone.

Then, I heard her get quiet. I could tell she was thinking.

"If you want an abortion, I'll help you, but shit is gon' get real bad with you and Big Mama. I would let you come home, but that's not a good idea, I think for the best of us, so you gon' have to tough it out over there, no matter what."

I was being given an ultimatum, and I knew it, even if she didn't say the words, I could hear it. I had to make a choice. Have this baby and just get over it, or I'd have an abortion and deal with Big Mama forever.

"I've been doing research, and I've got the

money. I just want this to al be over with."

"And what does jovon think about this?"

"I haven't told him."

"Lord, well, if you think you know what you doin', who am I to judge?"

"That's exactly right, who are you to judge. You're my mother, and I need your help. It's the least you can—"

"you need to remember I am your mother, and yes, it is the least I can do. It's all I'ma do, and you bet not tell Big Mama nothin'."

I looked at the phone thinkin' the same thing. While she was on the phone, I made an appointment to go to the clinic, and my mother said she would take me. I didn't know what was going to come of this, I just hoped Big Mama would forgive me.

Chapter 13 – Kimber

When I got to school, everyone was running up to me asking me questions about what happened with the fight. I didn't even think anyone knew, but of course, someone had recorded it and tagged me on Instagram, and the rest is history. I hated that things turned out this way. I really like Nick, but I didn't want to deal with his drama.

He made me promise to meet him after school to talk. I didn't have much time since I knew Big Mama was expecting me by a certain time, and if I didn't make it back on time, she'd flip her shit on me, and I didn't want to be bothered with that.

The last bell for school rung, and I couldn't have run out of school faster. I went over across the street to where there were picnic tables and took a seat. Nick showed up not too long after.

I rolled my eyes the second I saw him. I was so mad at him and I felt betrayed, I just didn't know what to do.

"Listen, I know what Jessica said probably got you pissed off, but that ain't even true—"

"Even if it ain't true, you obviously have fucked her in the past, not to mention you had her arm around her when I walked up on you, and you didn't even break up the fight!"

"You didn't look like you needed any help." He shrugged his shoulders. I shook my head and started getting up to walk away. Maybe Big Mama was right.

"Wait, Kimber, I get why you upset, and I'm sorry. Jessica and I don't have any kids together, and we never will. We did used to mess around, but I haven't seen her in years. I was just excited to see her, that's all."

"So, you think I'm boo the fool? You must think I'm one of those weak dumb ass bitches who just don't know any better. Get the fuck out of—"

SMACK!

My sentence was cut short by a smack being landed on my face. I just knew this had to be a dream.

"Are you serious right now? Did you just

hit me?" I asked, but it was a statement. I just got the fire smacked out of me.

"Hell yeah because you need to calm down. You might be able to talk to your other little boyfriends like that, but you can't talk to me lke that, baby.'

One minute, he was smacking me, and now, he had his hand on my face, rubbing where he'd smacked me. This nigga was trippin'. I didn't even have any time to argue, I had to get home before Big Mama did, or I'd be dead. All I could do was shake my head and walk away. Maybe I did need to stay away from Nick. He had too much shit goin' on, and I wasn't about to be lettin' him beat on me.

The walk I took to the house was much needed, and I made it with literally a minute to spare. When I got into the house, I went staright to the bathroom. Walking home always made me feel like I had to pee.

When I made it inside, I glimpsed myself walking to the toilet and couldn't help but notice the fact that my face was swollen from where Nick hit me. Was he serious?

There was nothing I could do to make it go away, which would mean I'd have to ignore

Big Mama, or else she'd snap. I still had a few minutes though before she'd be home, so I hurried and used the bathroom and came out, hoping to go straight to my room, but luck wasn't on my side.

The second I stepped out of the bathroom, there Big Mama was, looking me dead in the face. She looked up at me and grabbed my chin and turned it directly to the other side.

"You got into a fight at school?" she asked, her voice laced with disappointment.

"no, Big, just drop it."

"Ain't no just drop it. Who the fuck hit you? I can see their big ass hand print."

I knew if Big was saying fuck, she was pissed.

"Big, please, I just wanna—"

"Let me tell you something before you go," she said, grabbing my arms. "I got a feeling in my spirit it was that damn boy who ain't shit, and if that's the case, this all I'ma say about it. Get out now while you can, before a 'I was just angry' turns into your face looking like that permanently. I love you, and I know in a year you gon' be out the house, but you don't have to live this way, and I don't want you to. You're better than this, deserve better than this, and if I see him, I'ma beat his ass myself, since he like to put his hands on folks."

I busted out laughing. Even in the moment, something silly like that could make me laugh.

"I love you, Big," I said as I wrapped my arms around her.

"It's nothin'. Now go get yourself together so you can help me cook dinner."

I smiled and went to my room to change my clothes. I barely had my pants off before my phone started vibrating.

"I'm sorry...."

"Please, I didn't mean to snap like that..."

"Kimber, answer me. Come on, I know you ain't that mad for real."

I didn't even respond to the messages. There was no reason for me to. I had no intentions on ever going back to him. There was no way I was going to talk to a potential abuser. I would miss the dick though. He wasn't the only guy I'd been with, but he was the best so far. Too bad for him though.

Chapter 14 – Honesty

"You did what?" I turned my phone around to look at it. The last few weeks, I started talking to this new girl, Daisha. Once I had that talk with my aunt, I felt much better. I mean, it took me a minute to digest the fact that Brittany was moving on and had moved on, but once I got over that, I felt so much better, and somebody new came into my life.

Daisha was smart and outgoing, really extroverted, and she made me feel like I could be too, even though I knew that wasn't really my speed for real.

Daisha and I talked on the phone everyday, and she gave me more attention than I could have ever asked for or needed. She made me feel special and important, like somebody outside of my family actually cared about me. She cared about what I was going through and how I felt.

We went to school together, and we knew each other, but we didn't really know each other like that, not really. She came up to me at lunch one day and just started talking. If I wasn't sitting with Kimber or Saniya, then I sat alone, and I was on this day, but she just started talking to me, and I was happy to have the company.

Today, we'd been on the phone for hours, just like any other day. She was telling me about how she signed up for this extreme adventure course for the summer and she wanted me to do it with her.

"You know we black right, we don't get into that type of mess."

We both laughed, but the laughter was broken up by yelling. At first, I thought I was going crazy, but I knew I couldn't be. I would know Big Mama's voice anywhere.

"Honesty? You hear me?" I heard Daisha's voice on the other end of the phone, but that didn't have my attention.

"Yeah, let me call you back, ok?"

"Ok."

She sounded stale, but I'd have to call her later. I got off of my bed and opened the door to my room and looked downstairs, where Saniya was waving her arms at Big Mama. At that point, I couldn't even hear them because I couldn't believe Saniya was bold enough to act like this with Big Mama.

Kimber came flying out of her room, looking a little heavy, but I didn't know what that was about. I'd have to figure that out later too.

"What's the problem now?" Kimber asked me, and I was just as lost and as confused as she was. I shrugged my shoulder, and we both went to the top of the stairs to get a better listen. Aunt Lucinda was sitting on the couch, acting unbothered, so whatever it was, she already knew about it.

"So, first, you don't come home last night, and you think you can stay out, doing what? You were with Jovon weren't you?" Big Mama asked, her fists resting perfectly on her hips.

"No, Big Mama, I wasn't."

"Then where were you? You showin' up here today all tired. You gettin' high? You're a pregnant woman, you can't be gettin'—"

"I'm not high! What type of person do you think I am?"

"I don't know, I thought you were better than this, running all over town, doin' God knows what, with God knows who..."

I was just trying to figure out why I didn't know that Saniya had been gone all night. I hadn't come out of my room so far this morning except to go to the bathroom, and it's not like I kept tabs on everybody. I was finally able to live my life, so I tried to stay out of everybody else's way.

"You know what, Big Mama. I didn't want it to have to be like this, but I guess it does. I had an abortion, ok? I didn't want a baby, I don't want a baby, and I want to live my normal and regular life as a teenager. I messed up, but that don't mean I should be penalized for it for the rest of my life!" Saniya shouted.

Both me and Kimber almost had full heart attacks. We both gasped. I know I was super shocked from hearing that. I knew we could get away with a lot of stuff, but abortion wasn't one of them, and seeing Big Mama's face, I knew shit was about to get real.

"Who the hell would consent for you to get an abortion? You're not old enough for one legally!"

Everything in the room stopped moving. I wondered the same thing, I just prayed it wasn't Aunt Lucinda. But the way she was looking, I figured it wasn't her, thank God.

"Niya, don't tell me it was Jovon. He pressured you into getting one?" Big Mama asked, her eyes now full of sympathy.

"No, Big Mama. You not listenin'. I wanted this. It's my body and my choice, and you can either respect that, or—"

SLAP!

The shot heard round the world didn't have nothin' on what just took place. It was so loud, it was like the whole house broke.

My hand flew to my mouth I was so surprised.

"Let me tell you somethin', lil' girl, since you know so much. This world, that you so desperately want to be a part of and want to live in so bad, it ain't that great, and the world is cold. You went out and got an abortion, thinkin' you grown, but hid it from me, your auntie, and your cousins. Just because I don't approve of something doesn't mean I won't support you. Honesty, get down here. You too, Kimber."

My heart started racing. I didn't do anything wrong, and I didn't know anything about what Saniya had done.

Slowly, me and Kimber both walked down the steps, standing right in front of Big Mama.

"I don't condone this abortion, hell no. I think it's wrong. You laid down and got up pregnant. You should've handled your responsibility the first time, and you'd be ok. However, you didn't, but I could've gotten behind you. I would have supported you. You don't know what you doin' to your body and the stress and long term effects this might have on you later on in life. Honesty," she said, turning to me. I felt my heart drop into my stomach .

"I been knowin' you was gay your whole life, but I never once said I didn't love you nor have I ever stopped supporting you, and I never will. I love you. I can accept Honesty being gay, but I can't accept the fact that you went behind my back, made a decision that could ultimately change your life, and I don't even know what happened."

Tears started slipping from my eyes. I mean, I hadn't ever been girly, and it wasn't like I was floating around with boyfriends, but I didn't think Big Mama knew at all. Did Aunt Lucinda betray me?

"Auntie, you told her?" I asked, the words

almost a whisper. She shook her head.

"I would never do that to you. I would never hurt you like that."

I heard her words, but it was interesting to me that the one time I'd said it aloud to her, now Big Mama knew? No, that couldn't be right.

"I'll never trust you again! You were supposed to keep it between me and you!" I shouted. I had never felt so lied t in my life.

"Baby, your auntie didn't tell me—"

"You would take up for her. She's your daughter. We ain't never meant nothin' to anybody, not even to you for real, Big Mama. You want to keep us in the house and work us like slaves, it don't work that way. We have done everything you asked of us, but we're teenagers, we want to live too!"

I don't know where all this courage was coming from. Maybe it was because of what I just witnessed, but I honestly had grown tired of keeping my life a secret, and that was partially why I did because I didn't want Big Mama to find out and be upset. I'd been carrying the hurt and shame of who I was for so long, it felt good that the cat was finally out of the bag. It just didn't feel good the way it had to come out.

"You done lost yo damn mind too. You live here, for free. I don't treat y'all like slaves. I ask you to clean up after yourselves. Tell me why that's so wrong? I have neer asked you girls to pay a bill or really do anything you shouldn't be doing. Y'all in such a rush to be grown, but you get out there on your own, you won't know how to survive. I guarantee it!" Big Mama yelled. Looking at Saniya and Kimber, I could tell we were all thinking the same thing. That our hearts were broken.

"Y'all have given me hell since you got here, but I've taken care of you, loved you and been there for you the best way I know how. Maybe it's time II take my hands off you"

Big Mama threw her hands up in the air, and Kimber flew over to her. This was a side of her I'd never seen. I'd never seen her be the emotional one, so this was confusing.

"Big Mama, please, please. We'll do better, we won't get into nothin' else." Kimber was begging, and I didn't know why. I didn't want to stay here anymore. Big Mama's house wasn't the same.

Big Mama kissed Kimber on the cheek and then

let her go.

"Y'all can stay here if you want to, but I'm leaving. I'm goin' to Jovon's. At least he actually loves and supports me!" Saniya shouted before she went upstairs to grab her things. I couldn't believe the way this was all turning out.

"Kimber, Honesty, your parents are comin' to get you," she said, looking away from us.

"Why, Big? Why? Don't you love us?" Saniya questioned.

"That's exactly why I'm letting you go, so you can grow. I can't keep one and not keep all of you. Somebody is gona feel like that isn't fair."

She was right. We'd never really been separated, ever, and now, we were going to if we didn't get it together.

Saniyah shook her head and stormed off, heading toward the stairs. Our lives were falling apart right in front of us, and I didn't know what to do. I didn't want Saniya to leave, but I understood why she needed to. She was always one of the most mature people I've ever known, and now that she found her own way, I knew she was going to take it.

I looked over at Big Mama and Aunt Lucinda who both had tears running down their faces. They were devastated, and in a way, I was now too, and I didn't know how to handle what was taking place right in front of me.

That night, Saniya left, and she was no doubt going to leave. Kimber and I would have to go back home with our parents, and maybe that was for the best. Things seemed better before we got here. At least we didn't have any secrets between us.

"This little light of mine, I'm gonna let it shine, oh. This little light of mine, I'm gonna let it shine," I sang, looking out into the choir. When our parents came to get us, I told them I wasn't leaveing Big Mama no matter what, and I didn't care what was going on. I needed Big Mama, even if they didn't. I had someone else to think about now.

Two months had gone by, and Saniya was with Jovon, supposedly living "her best life". Her parents knew just about as much as we did. Every now and then she'd text and let me know she was ok, but other than that, I never heard from her.

Honesty went home, and she's seeing some girl named Daisha, who she really likes. I've seen her at school some, and she seems nice-ish. I don't know. I tried social media stalking her to figure out how she really is because I don't care what people say, social media can tell you a lot about someone's life, but so far, hers was full of pictures of her and honesty, and I had to respect that. At least she wasn't trying to hide my sister.

One month ago, I found out I was pregnant by Nick. I didn't want to reach back out to him because of what Big Mama said, but I was having his baby, and even though I wanted to ignore him and leave him alone, I couldn't. He blew my phone up every day until I told him I was pregnant. Now, it had gotten even worse. He would come and see me at home, school, work. The only place he'd let me have to myself was the church.

Big Mama told me that I would need a lot of help to raise my baby, and she was right, but also, thanks to my baby, I finally got verified on Instagram as a public figure and started making money through ads and sponsorships. Specifically for maternity items. I got trolls all day that said I was glorifying teen pregnancy, but that wasn't the truth. I was encouraging people my age. That was all I really wanted to do.

But now I'd found myself in church more than anything. At first, I thought everyone would judge me because I was pregnant, but everyone had really rallied around me and had been there for me. I liked having a support system. I didn't realize it, but I never really had one outside of Big Mama.

Church had become my sanctuary. It was the only other place outside of Big Mama's I felt comfortable, until right now.

After singing my last note, the choir practice crowd started clearing out, and I was about to head out the door until I saw someone in the back. I knew the frame, the body. It was Nick. How he found me? I would never know.

"What are you doing here?" I asked, my arms folded.

"You don't answer my phone calls or nothin'. You already showin', and I ain't spendin' enough time with you."

I crossed my arms and started patting my foot against the floor. This was a waste of time, and I'd done my best to become a better person. I got active in church, paid more attention in school, and I started acting more like a mother than a child, but Nick...he was out of control.

"You don't need to spend time with me. You can spend time with our baby once it's born."

"Once it's born? Ain't no way I'm not gon'

be spendin' time with my baby mama. For what? It's somebody else, ain't it? Man, everybody told me not to get with a Instagram hoe."

"Nick!" I shouted, pushing him out the doors of the church. He was really out of control. I'm not one to always follow the rules, but cussing on the grounds of church, I knew that wasn't right.

"Bitch, get yo hands off me," he said, pushing me away, knocking me to the ground.

A car pulled up. I could see it between Nick's legs as I was on the ground.

Then, I saw him lean over me, and I'm not gonna lie, fear shot through my body. Big Mama had been telling me for weeks now that he had a temper, a really bad one that would make my life harder. She said I should've never let him know about my pregnancy, but I felt like everyone deserved to be in their child's life. Now, I was starting to regret that.

A blow made it down to my face before I realized what was about to happen. I looked up, and Nick was being pulled backwards.

"Young man! I know you better put your hands up in the air before you get shot!"

I looked over, and Big Mama was talking to Nick with a gun pointed directly at him.

"Big Mama, no!" I yelled. Not because I wanted to save him but because I didn't want my grandmother to be out here like this.

"Baby, you alright?" she asked, looking down at me. At first, I felt like my ears were ringing, but now after a few seconds and maybe an adrenaline rush, I was able to get up.

"I'm ok, Big. Please, don't shoot him."

"Oh, I ain't gon' shoot him, today. Let me tell you somethin' young man. If you ever come around my granddaughter again, I will shoot you in front of God and anybody else who needs to or wants to watch. You understand me?"

He had his hands up in the air, and from what I could see, he seemed scared.

"I said, did you hear me?"

He turned around and looked back at me, and I heard Big Mama's safety come off of her gun.

"I hope you got a good look because you'll never see her again, and before you say anything, I know the whole police department, so I dare you to try to be in her life. This baby is well loved, and we don't need whatever evil it is inside of you makin' you put your hands on women. Now get out of here!"

I've never seen someone move so quickly a day in my life. I didn't think it would come down to this, and I didn't think I had to be on guard like that about him. What was it about Big Mama that she was always right?

"Come here, baby. Come here."

Big Mama opened her arms and I ran right into them.

"How did you know? How did you know he was…he was—"

I couldn't even finish my sentence if I wanted to. I couldn't muster up the energy to say aloud what really just happened to me.

"When you gon' learn that Big Mama got a direct line to God, and I'm old. You live long enough you pick up on things and learn to listen to God. That's all I've ever wanted for you and your sister and cousin. I love all three of you. I just wish Saniya would've listened to me."

That was something I wished too. Every time I talked to Saniya, I knew she was bullshitting about being happy. She was miserable, but she was also very prideful, and she wouldn't dare say how she was really feeling, even though I knew.

"Big Mama, don't worry about Saniya. She's always been the one who was on her own the most. Sh'es always been the most independent out of all of us, and if anybdody is gonna make it, it's gonna be her, ok?"

Big Mama nodded her head like she didn't believe me, but I had to have faith, right? That everything would turn out ok.

Had I listened to Big Mama from the beginning, even before when she told me about boys, I would've been better off. Now I was having a baby by an abusive man, who I could never love and would never love me. I didn't know anything about him. Big Mama always warned me about not paying attention and slowing down. We did want to be grown so bad that we missed the most important lessons she was trying to teach us.

My baby wouldn't have a father, but it would have an amazing great grandmother. My only fear was that my baby would grow up and hate me because of its father not being around, because no matter what, Nick had to be out of the picture. I had to take care of our unborn baby, even if that meant raising my baby without its father.

Big Mama grabbed my hand and led me to the car. Had it not been for Big Mama, I don't know what I would've done. She pretty much saved my life. I still had a long road ahead of me, but at least with her by my side, everything would be ok. Too bad my parents didn't know how to get some act right. It seemed like my grandmother and auntie were better for me than my own parents.

Chapter 16 – Saniya

"Bae, get up. Come on, get up," Jovon whispered in my ear. Just the sound of his voice annoyed my spirit. I didn't want him to be anywhere near me.

Living with a man was terrible. He was dirty, kept the new apartment that was literally moved into so we could live together just two months ago a mess. He never cooked, and I barely knew how. Not to mention, arguing with him was like talking to a child.

I thought having my independence would make me happy, but it didn't. Also having my independence meant that I had to make my own decisions and be an adult about the decisions that were made. My parents let me get emancipated. I'm just waiting for the final decision on that, but now, I somewhat wanted to take it back. I didn't want to live on my own, at least not with him.

I rolled over with an attitude.

"What is it?"

"Why you gotta wake up with an attitude every day? I haven't done nothin' but take care of you and love you. What's the issue? I even took you in after you killed our baby!"

Jovon got out of bed. His feet hit the ground and he headed toward the bathroom. We had a nice two-bedroom apartment, but I didn't care. I didn't want to be here with him. I wasn't ready to be living this type of life.

"Even took me in? I didn't even want to move in! The only reason I did was because I thought it was going to make you happy. I wanted to make you happy, but I didn't realize in wanting to make you happy, I was going to be miserable," I said, wrapping my arms around myself.

"Miserable?" jovon opened the door and shook his head.

"You don't even know what the beginning of miserable feels like. You dead ass killed our baby for your own selfish reasons. Some ole 'my body, my choice' bullshit, but you didn't think about how it would effect anybody else. You selfish as fuck!"

I ripped the covers off of my body hearing that.

"Selfish? Nah, I'll tell you what's selfish. Raising a baby I know I don't want is selfish. Bringing a child into this world without anything to offer it is selfish! So if I'm selfish for making the best decision for myself, then I guess I am selfish, and I'll be selfish all day! Again, I didn't even want to be here!"

I felt sweat dripping down my chest. I was so mad, my body was literally on fire I was so mad. He was out of the bathroom, getting closer to my face, and I was ready for war. I worked too damn hard for all the things I had for everything to turn out like this.

"If you wanna go, get out. Matter of fact, just get out. I don't care if you want to or not. I love you, but I'm not gon' be disrespected by you, Niya. Not for nothin."

I can't lie, I was shocked he was talking to me like this. Jovon got up and started grabbing my things.

"What are you doin'?" I asked, heading over to him.

"What you think? I'm gettin' yo shit together so you can go. You don't need me, don't want me, and you didn't want my baby. Just get out, Niya!"

Jovon was screaming so loud, my ears were ringing, and my head was starting to hurt.

"Fine, I don't give a fuck. I'll go, I'm ready to."

I started yanking my clothes out of his hands and threw them in the bags I came here in. I was on such a high, that I didn't think about what my next move was going to be. As I was getting my stuff, Jovon was behind me throwing my things down the stairs. He was upset, and so was I, but I was glad this was coming out. I still wanted to be together. I just didn't want to live in the same house.

I figured I'd give him a few days to calm down and then we'd be ok. I gathered my stuff and headed outside. I just knew he was going to stop me, but he didn't. Again, I figured he just needed some time. The only thing I needed to worry about was where I was going to go. If I went home, I'd break my father's heart. I'd already asked to be emancipated, and they agreed.

I thought the relationship between my mom and I was getting better, but it wasn't. Me asking to be emancipated only made things worse.

I hadn't really talked to anybody except Aunt

Lucinda, but I didn't know what I would say. I didn't want anyone to think I needed them, even though I did. I wasn't as adult as I thought I was.

Sure, I had a job, my own money, but I didn't have a car, a place to stay, and I'd burned almost every bridge with my family that had ever been built.

Sitting on the curb, I realized, Big Mama was right. I was in such a rush to become an adult that I'd pretty much ruined my life. Why would I do this to myself? I thought working a regular job and having some money in my pocket classified me as an adult, but it didn't, and that was made even more clear now by wanting to have an abortion so I could be my own person with my own life and live it as a teenager.

Jovon didn't come outside to check on me once, and I sat out there for two hours. But after those two hours were over and I started getting extremely hot, I did the only other thing I knew to do, and that was call Big Mama.

She'd always been there for me, and I was lucky to have her. I was nervous that she wouldn't come to get me, but the second she picked up the phone, she sounded concerned and like she still cared.

Not even twenty minutes after getting off the phone with her, she pulled up, hopping out of her car.

Tears poured down my face. I didn't know what to say except, "I'm sorry."

She smiled, tears coming down her face as well.

"I'm sorry, too, baby. Don't worry, you can come on home, and we'll figure this thing called life out for you. We don't need to go back and forth, ok?"

She wrapped her arms around me and kissed me on the cheek.

"I should've listened to you. I didn't want to be a baby mama, a wife, or...well, someone's house slave. I just want to be my own person."

"And you are. I love you, and you're an extraordinary person, but try living your life first and working for what you want. The rest will fall into place."

Big Mama always knew just what to say. I was always in good hands, I was just the last one to figure it out.

We got into Big Mama's car and drove to her

house. Pulling up to the front was the most refreshing moment of my life. I couldn't have been happier to be home.

Honesty chose to stay at home with her parents, and that was ok. She was doing the best out of all of us, and I wanted that for her, but me and Kimber? We needed our church singing, mean Christian grandmother to keep us on the straight and narrow.

Before we walked into the house, I stopped Big Mama and looked at her.

"I love you, Big Mama. I'll do better this time. I promise."

"I know you will, baby. You had to stumble a little bit to get it together. You human, and I love you too. Now come on so you can get yourself together. You need a shower," she said as she placed her hand on my back, laughing right along with me, as we walked into the house together.

The End....

Here's a list of books by me:

Flaws and all I love him 1&2 (Completed series)

This thug I love

The love we make 1&2

Mistletoes and hood love with a bow (Novella)

The love we make 3 (Drops this month)

Thots need love too (Collab drops this month)

Here's sneak peeks of my previous releases

Mistletoes and hood love with a bow

Chapter 1

Christmas

"Have y'all seen Lex? Silent, have you seen him?" I asked my sister who had been around this building at least twenty times tonight. Whenever she'd get nervous, she'd run at least a mile. Plus, it was a good warm up for her. This competition was supposed to be one of the biggest of my dancing career, so naturally, I wanted my man to be here to support me. He was supposed to already be here. I'd texted, called, FaceTimed, and did everything except put the bat signal out for his ass, and still nothing. I had no clue where he was, and I was tired of looking.

Lex and I had been together for the last three years. Up until recently, everything seemed to be going smoothly, no big issues. Don't get me wrong, we fight just like every other couple, but nothing that's too serious—not that I thought anyway, but this, not showing up to my competition? He must've lost his damn mind, and that, I just couldn't stand for. But right now, I had to get in the game, I had to be prepared. It wasn't just me competing—my two sisters, Holiday and Silent. As their big sister, I felt it was only right to make sure everything goes perfectly for them, well, as perfect as it can be.

Looking out into the crowd, I saw my parents. They had pride written all over their faces with smiles a mile long. I grabbed their hands and gave them tight squeezes.

"Y'all ready?" I looked over in both of their directions, waiting on them to answer.

"Shit, I don't know about y'all, but a bitch was born ready!" Holiday yelled, definitely getting the attention of the other dancers. She licked her tongue out at them, and I couldn't do anything but laugh because I already knew how she was when the pressure was on. It was Silent I had to worry about. She always felt like she had something to prove to me or to others that she was an amazing dancer, but that pressure was coming from herself. I already knew baby sis was cold; she just needed to know it herself.

I let go of Holiday's hand and put my hands on each side of Silent's face and looked at her.

"Look, we came here to do what we do best. What's that?" I asked, waiting for her to look me in the eyes. She'd had her eyes closed most of the time, calming her nerves. After a few moments of her not answering me, I rubbed my hand over her hair the way our parents used to when they were trying to get her to calm down. My mother and father were award winning dancers back in their day. They'd been on Soul Train, danced on the BET Awards shows, and toured with many artists together and separately. Dancing was in our DNA.

After a few deep breaths, Silent looked up at me and responded, "Dance till we drop!"

"And that'll never happen, so are we ready or what?"

Holiday had a personality of her own, and she was definitely a wild one, but I loved her nonetheless. The crowd was cheering out name, and it was time for us to step forward. I looked out into the crowd once again, and my best friend Lisa was coming in, finding her seat, I was about to wave to her when I saw that she looked like she needed to fix herself, like something wasn't right. She seemed...off. Her hair was all over the place, and her make up was a bit messed up. Her dress that she'd gotten custom made for the evening was running up her leg. That was odd to me, but Lisa was Lisa's business, not mine.

The music started playing, and as always, our signature move was ready to be executed. I always came out first, then Holiday, and then of course, Silent, each turning our heads to look at the other, and when I saw the look of confidence on Silent's face, I knew my sisters were ready to tear some shit up.

As the music continued going and we handled our portions of the choreography, I saw Lex. My heart started racing a million miles per minute with joy. I couldn't wait to wrap my arms around him, but something was off about this nigga, too. As I watched him tie his belt back around his pants, I knew I had to have been trippin'. There was no way I saw what I thought I saw. I'm not stupid by any means, and I'ma always put two and two together, but this time, if two and two equaled Lisa and Lex, they asses were as good as grass.

I focused back on the competition at hand, and Silent slid in with her final move, wowing the judges.

"Each of you are light on your feet, just like your mother."

"I love the uniformity and the signatures each girl has made for themselves. I love the sister act."

"Last but not least, each brings their own diversity and presence to the stage."

Holiday, Silent, and I smiled and jumped up and down. No matter how many good things people said about us, we always felt humbled by each judge's opinion, and it wasn't always without criticism. We waited for the judges to give our the final scores, and as we were standing there waiting, I saw Lex and Lisa staring at one another just a little bit too long, like they needed to talk about something or like they knew something I didn't, but I was definitely going to find out.

"Ten!"

"Ten!"

"Ten!"

Each judge announced our score, giving us another win under our belt. As happy as I wanted to be, I couldn't even muster up the energy to be happy because all I could think about was Lex and Lisa, and how I just knew they better not had been doing what I thought they were. Upon us winning, we were given a bonus check of $100,000, trophies, and a photo shoot to announce our win. Once we were given our earnings, I hugged my sisters, and we went back stage to change our clothes.

"Why you not smilin', bitch? We won!" Holiday jumped up and down and then started twerking in the mirror. I didn't give a damn about any of that...not right now. I put on a fake smile though, just for them so I wouldn't spoil how they were feeling even though I was dying inside to know the truth.

After a few minutes of us putting on our street clothes, I heard a knock at the door. I went to open it, and it was our parents, Lisa, and Lex.

My father hugged and kissed each of us, and our mother stood there with tears in her eyes.

"Mommy, why are you making that face?" Tears were threatening to fall. I got up from my chair and wiped the lone tear that she was doing her best to keep from falling of fher face.

"I'm just so proud of you girls. You know how to make your father and I proud, and you really did that today, but I already knew you girls were talented, and now, the rest of the world does too."

My mother and father and all of us joined in a hug, and then, I looked over at Lex and Lisa.

"Can y'all give me a moment with my man and my best friend? I wanted to share some news with them."

I had a devilish look on my face, but nobody picked up on it, and I mean nobody. My parents and sisters left the room. Before they left, I told them to go ahead and go to dinner, and I'd be there to meet them. It was always customary for them to take us out to dinner whenever we had a competition—win or lose.

"Bae, I'm so proud of you—"

I put my hand over his mouth, not wanting to hear the bullshit he was spouting. Lisa looked confused, and she walked up to me, smiling.

"Christmas, girl, you already know—"

"Alright, both of y'all shut the fuck up and listen. I don't know if y'all think I'm boo boo the fool or what, and shit, maybe I am since I NEVER thought my best friend would fuck my nigga—"

"Christma—"

"I said shut the fuck up, Lisa. Please, let me finish, and then you can say whatever stupid ass lie I'm sure you gon' tell.Both of y'all really got me fucked up. I mean, Lex, how did you think this was going to go between us? How could you do this?"

Tears then slid down Lisa's face, and I already knew what it was.

"Instead of whoopin' y'all asses like I really want to do, I'ma just let it slide. I really don't even have time for the fucker either one of y'all tryna put down, and I got better things to worry about than either one of y'all. Lex, I want your shit out of my house tonight, and I don't mean tomorrow, I mean tonight!"

Before walking out of the room, I turned back and looked at Lisa and shook my head. "And if you didn't know, you dead as fuck to me too!"

I then exited the room, heartbroken and betrayed, but I knew there had to be something better than this coming my way.

Chapter 2

Drusiel Gains AKA Dru

"Another win for Drusiel "The Muscle" Gains. Dru, how does it feel to stil be undefeated? Twenty fights, and you haven't lost yet?" a reporter caught my attention as I was leaving the ring. It was true, I hadn't lost a fight, and I didn't plan on it. Most people think boxers are aggressive and crazy, but I'm not. I learned to channel the stresses of life through boxing. I don't wanna hurt nobody for real, but aye, if you get in that ring, you better be prepared to fight for your life with me.

I smiled, noticing the crowd was still going wild. I finally gave my attention to the reporter who was walking along side me as I was going back to the locker room.

"Honestly, it's a blessing. My whole career is a blessing, and I'm thankful for everything I've been given. I'm thankful to my trainer, to my family, to my parents—to everyone who helped me along my journey, especially my brother and sister and best friend. Without my family and friends, and of course, the fans, I wouldn't be shit. Thank you!"

I raised my fists as I left the gym and headed to the locker room. As always, my brother, Blair, and my best friend Dakota, were waiting for me in the locker room.

"Bruh, I know I say this every time you do it, but damn! I can't even believe how you knocked that nigga out!" Blair gave me a hug, sweat and all. My little brother loved the hell out of me, and I loved him too.

"Aye, small things to a giant, right?" I smirked.

"Small things to a giant? Shut up, nigga. I'm just tryna see when you gon' come back in the gym and show yo face. You know niggas be surprised we so close, like we just that different," Dakota admitted. Dakota was my best friend. When his parents died, he came to live with us, so he's really like my brother. When he said he was gonna open up his own gym, I of course supported and helped him get business and clientele. My name alone rung many bells, but his story ain't mine—I'll let him tell y'all about that later.

"You right, Kota. So, what's up for tonight? Another win means y'all niggas owe me a night out. What y'all tryna do?"

"Shit, I'm tryna go out and get fucked up, what y'all tryna do?" Blair asked. His young ass knew he couldn't handle his liquor, but I let him make it.

"We can do that. Let me shower and change my clothes, and we'll head out."

I went and hopped in the shower, getting the sweat and blood off of me. I could wrap my hands up in the car, something I liked to do just to keep the swelling and shit down. You hit a nigga a couple of times, your hands bound to swell up on some real shit. After my shower, I threw on my clothes and asked where we were headed. Dakota and Blair said they'd seen a couple of bars on their way to the match, so it was only right that we bar hopped.

As soon as we got into the car, we were listening to music, you know, setting the mood. I wasn't really looking for anything but a good time. It had been a while since I'd been out, especially since I'd been training for this upcoming fight, but now, I had a little off time, and I wanted to enjoy myself.

We approached a bar; the flashing lights on the outside made it look like a stirp joint, and ain't no way I'm payin' to see a bitch get naked, when I could get that for free, and my boys knew that, so when they said bar, I knew they had to mean bar.

As soon as we hopped out, I was greeted by the people waiting in line. I had to give a couple of autographs and of course I'm always here for the pictures. I would never understood people who made their careers off the backs of others who didn't make time to take pictures and sign shit that meant the world to them. Without those people, we wouldn't be shit, so I always made time for them.

After we took a couple of pictures, I was ready to wait in line. I would never be so big that I thought the regular rules that went for other people somehow didn't apply to me. That just wasn't realistic to me, but before I could even get in the line, the bouncer tapped my shoulder and said, "The Muscle? Nigga, you ain't gotta wait in line. You comin' straight through the door. You too humble." The bouncer laughed, and I did too. I appreciated the special treatment, but I swear it wasn't necessary. I shook up with him and took a picture with him. Again, I love the fans. Me, Blair, and Dakota stepped into the bar, and it turns out that it was more of a club. The music was jumpin', and so was everyone else. The crowd was live, and there were bottle girls walking around with shots and drinks on their carriers.

"Aye baby, let me get one of them," I heard Dakota say. She smiled at the three of us and lowered her tray so we could grab the shots.

"How much I owe you?" I asked. She licked her lips, but I wasn't interested. Something about a woman who worked in a club always threw me off. Y'all can call me judgemental if you want to, but I always felt like they were messing with everyone in the club, and the special attention wasn't really special, if you know what I mean.

"Twenty-five dollars, please."

Money wasn't shit, so I didn't have a problem paying it; I just hoped they would be worth the money.

"To the night!" I shouted, and Blair and Dakota clinked glasses, and we threw the shots back. We made our way through the club on some boogie shit. Blair was a dancin' ass nigga, and he always had been, even when we were younger, so I let him get his groove on. Dakota had some girl over in the corner, and she was throwing her back up against him, and he had that look in his eyes like he was ready to fuck. I already knew what type of shit he was on, so I had to just let him be himself. I didn't mind groovin' alone. It was all good to me, until something started moving in the corner of my eye. Niggas were always tryin' me because I'm a boxer.

They think they can fight and beat me up, so I'm always on high alert. I turned around to see who or what it was coming in my direction, and it wasn't a what, but a who, and she wasn't paying me any attention.

Baby was fine as hell. Light-skinned, honey-tipped long dreads, high cheekbones, and a body to die for. She had a little booty, but it fit her body just right, and the way she was smiling while she was dancing turned me on. She had such a pretty smile, and she wasn't in here dressed like half of these other females in here. She had on simple harem jogger pants with a crop top t-shirt and some high-top Chucks. She was all that.

The music changed up a little bit, and I saw her and Blair getting close to one another. I already knew what was about to go down. My brother was a Youtube sensation. Everybody who was into the dance scene already knew him, so when the beat dropped, I knew they were preparing the floor for him. I didn't know who this girl was that was about to try to battle my brother, but I knew she was about to get shit jumpin'. I could tell by the way they were dancing, but I was surprised, because the way she looked, and the way she moved, I felt like she was on some classical dance style type stuff, but she was givin' my brother the business with the way she moved her hips, and her arms were winding around her body like a clock. She was all that.

The crowd was hype, and I of course was cheering my brother on. By the time the music stopped, they were both out of breath and smiling. My brother gave her a hug, and I wondered if he knew her. I made my way closer to the two of them and interrupted their conversation.

"OK, bruh, I see you ain't come to play."

Blair had sweat drippin' off of him but he laughed and said, "Hell yeah. I been waitin' on the opportunity to battle this girl. This is Christmas. She just won a dance competition tonight."

Christmas looked up at me and smiled. I returned her smile. "Hi, I'm Drusiel Gains. It's nice to meet you, Christmas."

"Likewise."

Blair looked at us, and he already knew what was up. "Look bruh, I'ma let y'all get up.

I'ma head over here and chill with Kota for a minute."

I nodded my head and gave my little brother a hug. Christmas and I stood still for a moment, just staring at each other. She then laughed.

"What's so funny?" I asked, wondering why she was giggling when neither one of us had said anything.

"I'm sorry, I'm a little drunk, and I'm tryna laugh to keep from crying for real."

"Crying? What a beautiful girl like you got to be cryin' about? You took home a W today from what I hear. Winners don't cry baby."

She laughed again, but then her smile quickly disappeared when she looked toward the door. I turned around to see what she was staring at, and a dude had walked in with another girl. From the look on Christmas' face, I could tell she knew them.

"You good?" I grabbed her arm, and she looked up at me. I ain't no punk ass dude, but touching her, something came over me.

"I would be better if I weren't here. I came here

to get away from them." She nodded her head in their direction.

"Ex boyfriend with a new girlfriend?"

"Something like that. Try was just my boyfriend a few hours ago and my best friend."

That was some foul ass shit, and even though I hadn't experienced anything like that, I could only imagine how she was feeling.

"So, you gon' leave because of this nigga? They wanna make you uncomfortable, don't let them win. Don't let them steal your win."

"You don't even know me, why you willin' to be all nice to me?"

I could tell she was clearly guarded from the situation at hand, but I was a good dude, and I had every intentions on showing her that. "Because youre a woman, and no woman should be treated like that. Just follow my lead."

I could tell she was hesitant, but when I stuck my hand out, she took it with a smile. I led her back out onto the dance floor, and we started dancing. The record changed to something slow and smooth. I grabbed her close to me, wrapping my arms around her waist. Her perfume was so strong, but in a good way. I could tell it wasn't that cheap shit—she looked like the type of woman to wear Chanel.

Her face brushed up against mine, and I distanced myself to spin her around so dude could see that she was being treated well in his absence. She giggled when her chest brushed back up against mine.

"How'd you learn to dance like this?" she inquired.

"You don't have a brother who knows how to dance and don't somehow learn a thing or two. I used to go with him to his dance classes and shit, and one of them was in traditional dancing. Plus, my sister is getting married next year, so she got us all on high alert."

"That's actually smart. Most men wouldn't want to do something like that."

"I ain't most men, Christmas. Speaking of which, your parents really named you Christmas? Like, that's not a dancing name?"

"Ha! No, my parents loved the holidays, so there's me, my sister Silent and Holiday. My parents were on one."

"Nah, they was on some different shit, and I can dig it."

As we were dancing and conversing, I could feel some eyes on me, like somebody was staring a hole into the back of my head. I turned around and looked to the right of us, and her ex was staring at us, watching enviously. I would be too. Christmas was fine as hell.

"Damn, dude really pressed behind you," I whispered into Christmas' ear. She looked over and saw him, but I could feel she was relaxed under my touch.

"You snooze, you lose, huh?" she said back, and I laughed.

We continued dancing until the song changed, and then she said she needed to use the restroom. I had been in clubs like this when shit went down with females and people wantin' to grab them in the bathroom or disturb their entrance and shit, so I couldn't let her go by herself.

"Here, let me escort you that way."

I grbbed her hand and led her through the

crowd, making sure she got there safely. I checked the inside to make sure to make sure everything was on the up and up, and then I came back out and stood guard of the door to make sure she was good. When she came out, she was laughing.

"What's going on now? Another cry to keep from laughing situation?"

"Nah, of course not. I'm just surprised how sweet you are. A protective boxer? Unheard of."

"Is it, and oh, you know who I am, huh?"

"Doesn't everybody?"

I shrugged my shoulders, and then I noticed she was swaying. Christmas was drunk as hell, and I wanted to make sure she was going to be ok.

"How you gettin' home? You drive?"

"I did, I got my keys. I'll be ok."

"Nah, ain't no way. How 'bout this. I had one drink. We can go get something to eat and then I'll make sure you get home. I'm not on no stalker type shit, but I wanna make sure you get home OK and safe. How that sound?"

She made a face, and I knew she wasn't comfortable, but there was no other option for her. I wasn't about to let something bad happen to her.

"What about your brother? Didn't you drive?" she asked, still swaying.

"I never drive to a match. Driving takes me out the mood, and I need to focus before it happens, so I rode with my trainer, and then my brother drove. He a grown ass man, he can take care of himself. Plus, he here with my best friend, Dakota. He'll be alright."

"Well...what did you have in mind for food? I could eat, and I know it'll help me sober up."

I nodded my head and grabbed her hand. I threw my hand up in the direction of Dakota and Blair and walked outside with Christmas. She pointed to her car, and I told her to wait on the sidewalk so I could go and get it. She had a nice little Mercedes, midnight blue with the chrome handles. I guess this dancing shit must've been lucrative for her. I turned on the car, scooting the seat back some to get my legs going and then pulled up. I got out of the car and went to open her door.

"A gentleman, too? That's really nice."

"Of course. This your shit, of course I'ma open the door for you, and again, you're a woman. You got it."

I grabbed her hand and helped her get in because she was so drunk. When we got in the car, Christmas' phone automatically connected, and jazz music started playing. I could vibe with it. It was two o'clock in the morning, and the only thing that was open was Waffle House. I pulled into the parking lot, and she had a smirk on her face.

"This is a good move!"

"The best move, baby."

I parked the car right in front of the building, and then rushed to the other side to get her out of the car.

"You sure you should be eating this? I don't want you to purge after you eat all this grease."

"I can eat this shit and pay for it tomorrow. I'm sure I'll find a way to get the extra calories off." I winked at her. I didn't mean it sexually, but it seductively came out anyway.

"Boy, come on and let's get some food."

I grabbed her hand and then opened the door with the other. We took a seat at the bar and ordered our food. Everybody knows what goes on in Waffle House. It's the place to be.

We sat there talking, getting to know one another as best as we could with the little time we did have. When the food came, we were still in the middle of our conversation, and it seemed like Christmas was on her way to finding herself sober. She wasn't swaying, and her eyes didn't look as glossed over.

After we were done, I pulled out my wallet. I saw Christmas reaching for hers, and I put my hand in front of hers. "Don't do that, baby. I got this."

"I can pay for my own meal, Dru."

"Yeah, you can, but you shouldn't have to, and when you're in my presence, you won't."

Christmas wrapped her arm around me and tilted her head on my shoulder. Having her against me felt so good. I hadn't been in the presence of a woman I actually liked in a long time, but I wasn't tryna rush and get married, but being around her was nice. After I paid and left a tip, we walked away and got into her car. She gave me directions to her house, and I told her when I got there I'd catch a Lyft back so she didn't have to worry about dropping me back off.

We arrived in front of her home in twenty-five minutes. I was lowkey dreading leaving her because I didn't know if I'd ever see her again and I wasn't going to ask for her number. If she wanted me to have it, she'd give it to me.

I turend off her car and went around to the side to let her out once again.

"Thank you for the night. You don't know how you saved my night for me. I don't know what's going to happen when I go in the house, but for tonight, I feel good."

"That's all I wanted," I said, as I brushed her dreads from her face, pulling them behind her ear to get a better look at her face. She was as beautiful as she was when I'd first seen her. I'm not a sensitive nigga, but the moonlight hittin' her face was just right.

She grabbed my hands and looked up at me for

a second, and I smiled. She then started to walk away, so I pulled my phone out of my pocket. I hadn't checked it the whole time I was with her, and I didn't have a need to, not when I was with Christmas. She kept my mind occupied with her conversation and of course, her beautiful face. I really like dhow she opened up to me about her nigga, well, ex nigga Lex and her backstabbing ass best friend Lisa. I could tell she was feeling me as much as I was feeling her, and I hoped one day, we would reconnect some type of way.

I was pulling up the Lyft app when I heard her drop her keys on the porch. I turned around, and she was throwing up all over her front porch. I slid my phone back into my pocket, laughing, and grabbed her keys from the ground and opened her door.

"Don't look at me, Dru. Just….just loo-"

I turned back around, and she was throwing up again, this time, on herself.

"Damn baby, you got it that bad, huh?"

Tears were coming out of her eyes, and I could tell she was embarrassed, but there was no need for that. Shit happens, even and especially when you don't want it to. Once the door was open, I picked her up. I ain't give a shit about no throw up. I get blood on myself all the time—throw up is just another bodily fluid. I carried her into the house and looked around. She was almost passed out in my arms. From the hallway, I could see a light turned on, so I followed it and carried her to her room. There was a bathroom inside, and she took straight off into it.

I sat down on the foot stool she had in her room and called out to her. "Christmas, you OK? "

"Just…give…me…a…second!" she shouted back. I could hear her tossing up everything in her stomach.

A few minutes later, I heard the shower turn on, and I knew that was my cue to go. I got up and was going to sneak out, but then she stuck her head out the door.

"Do you mind staying? I know I don't know you, but I really don't want to be alone, and from the looks of it in the closet, Lex did at least come and get his shit, so I'll be here all night. Will you just stay long enough for me to fall asleep?"

In a short amount of time, I had grown fond of her, and I didn't want the night to end anyway, so of course I agreed.

"Yeah, go ahead and handle your business. I'll go wait in the living room for you."

The door closed back and I made my way back into the living room. I could tell this house was all her. From the ceilings to the floor, I could tell she'd decorated this whole place. I wouldn't have even known she had a man had it not had the stinch of a nigga or a few of his items left inside the house. I scoped out the kitchen and then the dining room. I even looked at the pictures she had of her family on the wall. There were so many pictures of her and her sisters, I could tell she was close to them the same way I was close to Blair and Dakota.

After a few minutes, she came back out with her robe and bunny slippers on. Shit was cute as fuck. Her dreads were tied up in a bun, and she was smiling.

"Feeling better?"

"Like a brand new baby. Sometimes, you just

gotta get that shit out, you know?”

“Oh, I know exactly what you mean.”

She came around the couch and took a seat. “You wanna find something to wach on Amazon Prime?”

“Yeah, we can do that.”

She cut the TV on, and the first thing on was a recap of my match. “We ain’t gotta watch that.”

“Sure we do! I missed the match. I haven’t missed one in a while.”

“So, you a fan?” I smirked, turning around to look at her.

“I didn’t say all that, but I’m up on the shit. Now hush, let me see what you was doin’ tonight.”

We sat back on the couch and watched. I normally hated seeing myself in a recap, but with Christmas, it was cool. “That’s probably why you’re a good dancer, you have good footwork.”

“Check you out, paying attention.”

She laughed and hit my shoulder. I grabbed her and started tickling her. It felt so natural with her, I couldn’t help it. I pinned her down on the couch, and her legs were kicking. Her laugh was so infectious, it made me laugh too. She was turning her head, and her dreads got loose. They fell over her face, and I loved looking at it, so I moved them out the way. In that moment, she just looked so angelic, so perfect, I couldn't help but to kiss her.

Her lips were so juicy and wet. As soon as I kissed them, it was like having a drink of water. I was thirsty for her. Her arms reached around my neck, and my body fell into hers perfectly. I grabbed the sides of her long legs and wrapped them around me. She pulled me in as close as she could. I could smell her body wash and it meshed well with her natural body scent.

I pulled away from her feeling the moment getting too heated. She'd just got out of a relationship, and I didn't want to be some type of rebound sex, but when I stopped, she gave me this innocent look, like she didn't want me to, and I knew then, I was about to take baby down. I leaned back on top of her and started kissing her again. I'm a fighter but an affectionate nigga too. Her fingernails were scaling my back, lightly scratching me, and that shit had me turned on.

We both were breathing like dogs in heat, and I couldn't stand her breasts poking my chest through her robe. I had to see what she was working with. Slowly, I untied her robe and let it fall off of her. She was butt ass naked underneath, and her body was just as nice as I knew it would be.

I trailed kisses down her cheeks, then her neck, and then my mouth found her nipples. Her breath sped up, and I sucked her titties like my life depeneded on it. I used my left hand to squeeze the other as her body started grinding up against me. She wanted the dick, and I wanted to give it to her.

"Take me into my bedroom. Pick me up like you did to carry me in the house," she whispered.

"You liked that shit?"

"I loved it…"

I licked her bottom lip and sucked on it, and then carried her to the back for a night neither of us would ever forget….

the alarm went off and I knew it was time to leave. After one night part of me wanted to stay and hold her beautiful ass until she understood her worth. i couldn't do that I had shit to do. I slid my clothes on and left my number on her night stand and placing a kiss on her forehead before leaving out. Shawty was special. A blind man could see that.

Flaws and all I love him

Chapter 1

Nijay

"Stop, stop, stop, how are you singing about love and never have been in it? You're telling a lie when you sing this song and I don't believe you! Sing to me from here," Lisa, my singing coach, preached to me while pointing to my heart. She wasn't lying; I was nineteen years old and never had a boyfriend or a real kiss that I, at least, could count. I was average but, to others, I was a supermodel. I was dark chocolate with deep, dark brown sepia eyes, slim build, size 3 with a little booty, and breasts to match. I was a tomboy; I loved my sweat pants and my half shirts and shoes. I mean, I could wear heels, but they wasn't my cup of tea.

I was so excited about going on tour; not only was I going with my favorite cousin, Si-auni, but I was also going with the hit group Illusion. I had met the lead singer, Zaine, when he confronted me about a duet. At first, I was nervous, probably because I had the biggest crush on him, but then he had some dope ideas that I just had to be a part of it. We were making the video for our new song, *Can't Be Me Without You*. Originally, it was my song, but Lisa was right. I needed love or someone to show me the idea of a great romance.

"Try it again but, this time, try pretending

no one is in the room; allow the beat to speak to you. This time, I'm placing it on instrumental. I want to hear the words. Tell me a story, allowing me to connect with the song," Lisa demanded, placing the video camera on record and leaving to check on her kids. At first, I found it weird that she insisted I record myself but, after watching the tapes, I saw for myself what a lot of people was talking about. Don't get me wrong; I always put on a show but, when I'm alone, I amazed myself. Playing the instrumental, I opened my mouth, hoping I believed the words I had wrote.

"I can't stop loving you, after all the things you do to my heart. And we're out of control, but I can't let go of you. I wish it was simple darling, but we're playing a dangerous game. I thought we were over all the mistakes. These tears I cry telling me don't say goodbye, but what's a girl left to do, oh baby." I sung as if I was standing on the line between me and my man, deciding if I should stay or go. I never even heard Siauni walk in the room.

"That was great boo and the song is hot, but where is the sex appeal? I know you used to being on your soulful ish, but you need to channel Beyoncé's, *Cater To You*. The song is about loving a man who sees all of you and balance's you out, but you're standing there mouthing lyrics," Siauni said, waltzing in on my rehearsal like she owned the place, with her annoying behind.

"How do I be sexy with a guy when I don't even feel sexy? Maybe Zaine should do the duet with you instead," I countered.

"Not happening; why don't you start by stop acting shy and get to know the real Zaine, instead of making assumptions? What's the worst that can happen? You might find out that you have a lot in common. I've known you my whole life and the closest person to you is me. Don't you want to feel what real love is? Or what genuine affection is? Stop being timid Jay; I see you! When are you going to let others see it too? Because the girl I see is pretty amazing, if I do say so. Our tour starts tomorrow. Are you ready to show divas that new queens have arrived?"

"Of course I am. I dreamed of this for so long and here it is." We were both successful single artists and, now, we're about to drop the best combination CD anybody had ever heard. Honestly, this was the biggest gamble I made since my career started. I mean, don't be fooled. I was more in the Jill Scott type of music with a Whitney voice and my fans loved that, but my team and Lisa thought I should change it up and become versatile, trying pop and hip hop. At first, I shut it down because I wasn't used to change. I needed to have faith that this was my time; yet, most days, it was hard to believe. "I am ready," I said, coaching myself as I always did.

"Me too, for sure! Who would have ever thought two foster kids from Manhattan would be burning up the charts?" Siauni asked.

"Girl, a lot of people came from where we came from and represented. It's never about where you're from but where you're going. As long as my voice doesn't crack and my legs work, I'm going to hustle and sing my life," I proudly said.

"That's what I know. I'm so hungry and determined for the spotlight; I refuse to give up on something meant for me. For instance, like you and Zaine's duet." Si was right. We made chemistry when we sang and, because of my fear, I kept doubting myself.

I was dead beat tired. I was so much of a perfectionist that I would be in the studio for hours, trying to lay down a track or dance steps til I was satisfied. Music was my natural high. I wasn't me if I couldn't sing. After 9 hours of constant bickering, I headed home. Being as though I didn't live but ten minutes away, I got there instantly. Upon entering my apartment, I ran me a bubble bath and relaxed in my whirlpool tub. The craziest thing was my home was where I felt comfortable, but it was lonely. Besides me, the only friend I had was my dog, Queen. Now that the tour was about to start, she would be at the kennel til I return home. I needed a life. At 19, I was supposed to be out living it up; instead, I was in this big ole apartment by myself. I let the water out, turned on the shower, and let the water rinse all the soap off my body. After, I put on my skin softener and grabbed my flannel nightgown, instantly sliding it on.

I walked to the kitchen and poured me a glass of wine. I wasn't a heavy drinker; in fact, wine was about the only thing I could handle. I relaxed, thinking about my first encounter with Zaine eight months ago. I was recording and he happened to be walking past. Apparently, he was working on a solo project. For the life of me, I couldn't write this song, which was super crazy because I never had a problem before.

"I been in the dark space playing a fool. Running around, chasing lawd knows who. My heart's been broken from the tears I cried. Don't know how I'm standing when I feel so empty inside. Now you're standing here, saying you're not like my last and my feelings saying stay within my grasp. I wanna trust you and dive in, cause there's no me without you. But it's not that simple to let go of all I ever known."

"Why isn't that simple? It's crazy how your songs touch on so many feelings, but word around town is you never been in love or had a boyfriend. So, tell me, Ma, who broke your heart to make you feel so deep in pain?" Zaine asked, entering in my session without so much of an invite.

"*Excuse me, Zaine! I don't recall saying you can come in.*" I was giggling at the fact he was so bold and confident. He always was, since I met him. We hosted quite a few gigs when I started the industry, but didn't really get close til the night at the studio. It was a job, not a black people meet. I collected my check and went home, no more, no less. The music industry was full of makeups and breakups, and I just refused to be the next.

"*I heard your song; it's cool, could be better tho. How about we do a duet? You already released this version about heartbreak; now, make one about taking a chance. The way I see it; you need to sing about what you don't know, and you can't write about a happy relationship because you faking by putting me in the friend zone. Let me show you some good stuff.*"

Disregarding my last comment, Zaine walked in the booth, letting me hear his version. It was more upbeat and sexual but nice. After feeling him out and calling our managers, we worked out the final kinks and laid the track down. I never laughed as hard as I did with him. Things flowed naturally.

"*Do you know how beautiful you are?*" *Zaine asked, causing me to blush.*

"*People say it all the time, but I don't see it. I'm too much of a tomboy,*" *I responded. No matter who told me about my looks, I always took it as someone trying to be nice. In private with my cousin Siauni, I learned about makeup, clothes, and heels. Although, I wouldn't be caught dead outside in it. I was too self-conscious. I wanted to be thicker. No matter what I ate, I was always skinny, just like my momma.*

Zaine stood up, walked over to me, and lifted my head up while grabbing my chin. I always kept my head down, as if I was scared to speak and, in a way, I was when it came to him. I always allowed my doubts to scare me into not trying things.

"*My favorite painting is the Mona Lisa because to many, it's just a painting of an ugly woman. To me, her eyes tell a story, her clothes represent her body, and her smile warms my heart.*"

"*You calling me ugly, Zaine?*"

"*Nah Ma, the opposite. I'm saying your*

beauty is envied by others and different to some, but you're the only one you have to please. Be yourself. Stop comparing yourself to others because what you got, niggas want. Why are you afraid to get to know me? When we were hosting, the only conversations we had was what the tele prompter read; every time the event was over, you would high tail your ass out there before I could invite you out? Wassup with that?"

"Most girls lose themselves in the industry, so I put walls up to protect myself. Those events were a job; plus, I didn't want to get hurt behind another bad boy," I responded, putting my head down.

"Yo, on the real, I'm far from a bad boy. I don't mess around with singers or none of that. I only want to get to know you. If it's friends, cool, but stop making excuses to protect yourself."

"I don't want to get hurt Zaine."

"Look at me; in your heart, do you feel I would hurt you?" he asked, lifting my chin again while staring me down.

"No."

"Because I'm not, think about it. I'm out; my

mom's got an appointment. Hit me up and let me know how they love our song." Nodding and agreeing to meet up later in the week, I went back to my music.

Chapter 2

Saint

"Why can't I go on tour with you, Saint? What's different now than the other times I went with you? Oh! I see, it's cause Nijay and Siauni going, isn't it? You ain't shit and I put up with it because I love you. Not once in the three years we've been together have you said it back," Keri complained. She was worried about the wrong things. I couldn't tell her I loved her when I didn't. The only reason we were still together was because she could cook and was beautiful beyond words; yet, she was vain and self-absorbed. Most of the times, I thought she was with me because of what I could do for her. That's why I could never give myself to Keri whole hardheartedly.

"You sitting here worried about them, instead of us. Last tour, you was grinding up on Ne-Yo like some damn groupie. Where was the respect huh? You love me tho. I can't do this no more with you; when I come back, I expect you to be gone." I knew I hurt her feelings, but she had changed. I constantly cheated on her cause she allowed it. Always saying she was my wife, but what wife you know sharing they husband?

"Really Saint, after three years? It's always music this and music that with you, or the group got to practice, and let's not forget the mighty Zaine, who always need you, but what about me? All I wanted was attention and you couldn't even give it until I was entertaining the next man. I gave up my life and dreams so you could have yours. What am I supposed to do without you? I can't, please," Keri boldly stated while tears were filling her eyes.

"Keri, I never asked you to do that. You're not the same girl I met years ago. What you call attention, I call desperate Ma. When I was in the spotlight, so was you. I was never afraid of letting you shine, so don't blame me for that. Stop surrounding your life around men. Find out who you are because this is not you. I'll be gone for 8 months; that gives you plenty of time to be gone and I'll still put money in your accounts til you find something," I responded.

"I don't want your money. You can keep it!" Keri shouted as she got on her knees to suck my dick.

"Naw Ma, not this time," I stated and I kissed her forehead, then left out the door while a tear fell, not because I was a bitch but, as I man, I been saw the signs. Instead of letting her go, I was being selfish. In the industry, people are easily destroyed by fame. Keri was ambitious and had dreams of being the next Lisa Leslie, until she blew out her knee. Letting life consume her, she gave up. No matter what I did, it still wasn't enough. I always felt like I owed her for holding me down. She used to say that all she wanted was my heart, but being with her never felt right. Three years and it felt like a partnership rather than a relationship. I hoped she found the love she couldn't find in me.

I was not going to lie; I was excited. I loved Nijay and Siauni's music, and they were sexy as fuck. I'd known Nijay for about two years now from hosting gigs, and she was like my little sister. Her cousin Siauni was also in the industry, and we crossed paths here and there. I thought she was beautiful but, as a man, I wouldn't dare act on it knowing I had a girl at home. Despite the situation, Keri didn't deserve to be disrespected like that because I was raised to be a better man. Besides basic stuff about Siauni, I really didn't know her well. Granted, they were hit on constantly by men that they shut everything down and, truthfully, I could understand; I just wanted things to change on this tour for the better. Between the rumors about Siauni and what Jay expressed to me, it made me curious about her; I wanted to find out what she was about. The way Jay talked about her intrigued me. I knew for sure that she hated dating anyone in the industry, and the tabloids reported her dating Reggie Bush's wack ass, knowing damn well he couldn't handle her ass. He couldn't even hold onto Kim's ditzy ass.

Pulling up at the airport and boarding the plane, I saw her. I mean, I knew what she looked like, but pictures didn't do her justice. Siauni was a 5-foot-4, red bone, slim waist, plump bottom, with doe eyes and fuck me lips.

"Can I join you or is this seat taken?" I asked, sounding nervous.

"Actually, it is, but there are plenty of

seats over there. Why don't you go find one?" she asked, winking at me.

"You cute ma, so I'm going to let that smart shit go since you going to be my wife and have my kids someday."

Taking a seat across from her, I looked at her. I wanted a female who would match me in every way and the way she shot me down turned me on. I was nowhere near an ugly dude. I was 5 foot 9, brown-skinned, muscular build, with deep brown eyes and big wild hair. My body was full of tattoos. Never in my 23 years on this earth had I been told no, until now. I had 8 months to make her mine, so she could sing and ride me at the same time. I wanted this girl in the worst way. I was going to get her and I felt sorry for the niggas tryna come behind me because I was going to spoil the shit out of my wife.

Chapter 3

Siauni

Omg!!!!! Why is this man so damn fine? From his appearance to his voice, everything screamed boss. I didn't need him though. Money, I got it. A nice thick pole to scratch the kitty whenever I'm horny, got that too. Like I said, I didn't need him, but I wanted him in the worst way. I knew all about Saint and his situation with Keri, thanks to my cousin and, of course, rumors. We actually met a few times. I was not going to bash her; she was beautiful and so was I. The thing was, you had to have more than looks and that, unfortunately, was where Keri always fell short. I used to peep game all too well at how Keri would watch us, as if I would be moving in on her territory. We all worked in the same industry, so we always crossed paths. I was woman enough not to act off my emotions. The media stayed making false accusations, like the recent one that I was dating football player Reggie Bush, which was absurd when he wasn't even my type.

"Hey, big bro, where are Zaine and David

at?" Nijay asked while walking to her seat after hugging Saint, as I rolled my eyes. She stayed clowning me about how that was my bae. I wasn't going fake though. After being around him, if the circumstances were different, lil daddy could get it.

"David and Zaine will meet us in New York; their mom had her last round of chemotherapy and they didn't want to miss it," Saint replied.

"I'm glad she's doing better. We talked about it briefly when we were in the studio, about who inspired us in music and he said his mom," said Nijay.

"Actually, she's not doing so well. But after all the studies and tests, Ms. Emma was tired and restless and seeing her fight so that Zaine and David could be happy. Eventually, they agreed to let things run its course. She will meet us in Miami."

I sat in my seat taking in all that I heard. Jay and I were orphans. My dad left before I got a chance to know him and my mom was a drug addict who sold me over a bag of weed. Jay's mom died giving birth to her and her dad was doing a bid upstate for murder. I kept money on his books and talked to him often. He raised us both until we were thirteen. I knew the news of Zaine and David's mom hit home because they were just as close to their mom as we were to her dad, Air. His leaving took a toll on her; she blamed herself for him being in jail. I wished she would stop being stubborn and go see him. This situation proved that tomorrow's never promised to anyone.

As Nijay, finally took her seat next to me, I just stared at her. I wished my mother chose me over her drugs; however, that was not the case at all. Jay was lucky she had Uncle Air, who was there for her and always kept his promise. Whereas, I had constant disappointments. If it wasn't for Uncle Air stepping in to save me from my mom selling me for a bag of weed, I don't know where I would be. Hearing all my life that it was harmless always made me angry because, even then, nobody understood what I went through. I silently always hoped that she would walk through the door a changed woman. That never happened. I was fortunate, unlike so many others; they were there for me. Jay was my cousin, but I called her my sister and bestfriend because of how close we were.

"I know what you're thinking and no," said Jay.

"Your dad is up for parole and you can support him. That night wasn't your fault. When Drake kidnapped you and you pulled that trigger and killed him, you were only defending yourself. Don't you see your dad gave up his life, so you could live?" They gave him eight years for self-defense and he already served six.

"I know, but I can't seem to get past it all. I really miss him. We shouldn't have been in the house that night. I think about that night all the time, as if it haunts me. How could he play dad like that? What made him do that to me, to us?" Jay questioned, but I couldn't answer. Often, I wondered the very same thing.

"That's something you have to ask him and, unfortunately, Drake's not here to answer that for you. Jay, you got a second chance at life that night; stop wasting it on wishes and go follow your dreams."

"I miss him; what if my dad doesn't want to see me?"

"You know where to find him. Stop being scared; that's your dad. His love for you will never falter," I said before drifting off to sleep. I woke up feeling a little better. My dad was a touchy subject for me and Jay knew that; yet, a lot of the things I was saying were true. She was being childish, only because it was not her fault that Air went away. I always wanted the type of relationship she had with her father; only thing was my father was a no good piece of shit. My mother Jacey was my Uncle Air's little sister before he disowned her for trying to sell me before I entered the world, and my dad wasn't any better. He was a low level worker named Suryah. As a father, it was his duty to protect me; instead, he was down with the arrangements. At least that was what I heard over the years. Knowing they wasn't supposed to interact caused Uncle Air to force his hand by cutting off his drug supply, not allowing his contact to sell or buy products. Realizing what happened, he left, leaving me to never meet him. We only knew the stories because our hood was like 411; everyone knew something.